HEART

STEFAN TAYLOR

Heart

Copyright © 2021 by Stefan Taylor

Edited by Amanda J Spedding

Cover and layout: David Schembri Studios
www.davidschembri.net

ISBN-978-06486677-4-2

www.facebook.com/Stefan-Taylor-Authorscreenwriter

Published by Stefan Taylor

S

Melbourne, Australia

AUTHOR'S NOTE
TRIGGER WARNING

T hose familiar with my previous releases will know, that while they were entrenched in the Horror genre, they were written for a young adult audience.

HEART is **NOT** a horror novel. However, it does contain themes of sexual abuse, domestic violence, bigoted language and racial profiling. It also contains scenes of combat sport violence.

These themes may be upsetting or triggering to some readers.

The author further recommends that this book may not be suitable for readers under the age of sixteen.

Contents

CHAPTER 1

T he buzz of the alarm kicked her out of a deep, dreamless sleep. Ila slipped out of warmth and comfort, and into another day. Silencing the alarm, she lay back and swiped through her socials. A video grabbed her attention, and she sat up to peer into her phone's neon glow.

The video was a slick production showing men and women battling it out in the Octagon cage. Kicks, punches and grappling competitors brawling in modern gladiatorial combat.

The words: *Warrior Heart, MMA tournament,* blazed across the screen along with the caption, *Ten Thousand dollars in prize money!*

She'd been seeing this video a lot in the past month. Warrior Heart was a new tournament set up to give local combat athletes a path to the big time.

Ila allowed herself a moment of fantasy. A vision of herself stepping into the Octagon cage accompanied by the roar of the crowd, played out like a film in her mind. She imagined the elation of having her hand raised in victory while standing in the centre of the cage.

The video ended; the phone's screen went black. Ila

returned to reality with a mental bump.

She swung her legs out of bed in the silence of the morning, toes rubbing on the thick carpet, and her hands clutching the side of the mattress. She sighed sleepily. Reality was cold and drab this morning. Just like every other morning.

At least it was consistent!

The days felt so long, work or university, then training, and sleep. Rinse and repeat. Seven days a week, three sixty-five a year, for… well… at this stage it felt like forever. But she knew nothing lasted forever.

Ila realised she was drifting back into the beautiful silence of sleep. Warm and inviting. It would be the easiest thing in the world to simply, turn off her phone, lie back and drift off. If her mum checked in on her, or rather *when* her mum barged in, and ordered her out of bed, she could just feign sickness.

Just one day off the grind. One day! That wasn't too much to ask, was it?

She allowed all these minor fantasies to play out as she stood from her bed, moved to her closet and retrieved her Gi. She tossed the martial arts garment on her bed, and then reached for her belt. Ila clasped it lovingly, as if it were a newborn baby. It was an amusing thought. How could a three-meter long strip of cotton and nylon, dyed purple, mean so much to a person?

Folding the belt, she laid it respectfully on her Gi.

Rubbing her eyes, she moved to her small bedroom window where she was greeted with their neighbour's rickety back fence. Beyond the fence stood the twenty-storey Housing Commission flats.

The brutalist structure stared down on her solemnly.

The windows were a thousand watching eyes; waiting to see her next move. This monolith stood as a constant reminder of where she was, and who she was.

Beyond the flats, the sky was a clear sapphire.

There was another world beyond the flats. One she stepped in and out of. It was akin to dipping her toe in a cool pond on a roasting hot day.

Sometimes the flats stood as a guardian, trying to block her escape. Sometimes, as she returned from that other world, the flats marked a welcome site. Beneath the building's gaze, lay her home, for better or worse.

Ila flicked on the bedroom light, instantly snuffing out the mystique of the morning. She folded her Gi and belt into her gym bag, while taking a mental note on the day a head.

Friday.

This meant helping her mum get the young ones to school. A shift at the supermarket followed by two hours of training at the gym. Then she'd be studying until she literally couldn't keep her eyes open.

A thud on her door caused her to jump. "Ila! You up?" her mother's broken English seemed to rattle the house.

"Yeah, Mum, I'm ready!"

"Humpf!" she could almost see her mum giving a solid nod of approval behind the door. "Well hurry, time to move! Embrace the day that God sends you."

"Yes, Mum." She looked back to the flats and their thousand staring eyes. *'Listen to your mother, girl,'* they were saying. *'Get up and get out there!'*

"All right, I'm going," she replied with a yawn to the thousand eyes.

But for a beat, she stood and took in her reflection in her closet mirror. She'd put on some size in the last year or so. The constant training had seen her shoulders fill out and her brother kept calling her 'tree legs'.

Her face wore a few minor scars from stray elbows, and the odd accidental headbutt, yet her dark skin hid those well.

Cuts and bruises were part of the Jiu Jitsu journey. She gave her neck a solid crack, and felt the wave of relief flow down her back. Apart from the knee pain, neck pain and the odd shoulder dislocation, training was treating her well.

She smiled down at her purple belt, with the white tips, before zipping her gym bag shut.

The whole day was just a bridge to training. Her reflection smiled, giving her a nod of approval. Apart from the huge bags under her eyes, Ila thought she was carrying it all pretty well.

Tying back her shoulder length braids, she snatched up her gym bag, and stepped out into the hallway.

The battle against the day had begun.

*

Her mother barked something at Ila from the kitchen about waking her brother. Ila nodded vaguely and headed for the bathroom. All she could think of was training, getting out on to those mats and rolling against the others.

But that would have to wait because as the eldest at twenty-one, she had responsibilities. And they hung around her with the weight of a convict's chain.

"Ila! Get Mo and Evie ready, or we'll be late!"

"Yes, Mum," she called flatly back.

The chain dragged her forward.

Wrangling Evie and Mohammed into their school uniforms, she guided them into the cramped kitchen table to force some breakfast down their throats. The twins were born in Australia, and although they were only six, they spoke clearer English than their parents.

Their mother would often curse at them in the language of her home country, but this only caused the twins to cackle hysterically.

Her father was seated already in the same slumped position she found him every morning. Looking older than his fifty-two years, Amir sat with remote and distant eyes, staring at nothing and gazing inward to his own thoughts.

Ila wasn't blind; she understood the root of her dad's wistful sadness.

Sudan.

He missed his home country. Despite fleeing the wars, she knew he longed to be back there, feeling the baked earth beneath his feet. She couldn't pinpoint how she understood the cause of his pain. However, she felt it, and knew it to be true.

Toast was buttered, and jam was spread. She laid it in front of him.

He offered the slightest of glances, his hand touching hers in thanks. Then he returned to whatever memories were playing in his mind.

Realising her mother was speaking, Ila snapped to attention, and became aware of the pounding on the door.

"Ila! Get the door? And wake Abdul! How can that boy sleep so late?"

Her eyes went to the clock on the hallway wall. It was only just seven am, and too early for one of her dad's friends to be visiting. Maybe it was one of Abdul's hood-rat mates, looking for him. Heading down the hall, she banged on her brother's door as she passed it. "Abby! Get up! We gotta go!"

Yanking open the front door, she gasped in astonishment. Her brother, Abdul stood before her. Head hanging, his bright brown eyes gave her an odd, almost dismissive stare.

The two policemen stepped in beside Abdul.

"This yours?" the officer asked, grabbing Abdul's shoulder and half dangling him in front of her.

"Abby?" Ila couldn't hide her disappointment. He was here again, in the same situation he always seemed to end up in. Folding her arms, she stood tall before the burly men. It was her attempt at giving some sort of air of control over the cops.

They gazed back with hard, disinterested eyes that said, 'I hate doing this shit, but also love doing this shit' at the same time.

Only cops could give that look.

"Is my brother under arrest, *officer*?" She said the last word with a mock degree of respect, which wasn't lost on the young constable.

He gave a knowing smile and shoved Abdul into the house. He stood next to her like a dog that had been caught in the kitty treats.

"Nah, not too serious," the cop said with a yawn. "Seems Abby, had himself a big night. Few too many beers in the park with the boys." He turned to his partner. "Looked fun, didn't it?" he said flatly.

The lead cop's expression changed as Abdul stared at him. She felt the growing tension in her brother.

Despite being blessed with the height common in most Sudanese men, he was of such a slim build that even Ila, a good head shorter than her brother, could out muscle him.

The officer's grin widened. "Hope you're not thinking of adding some more serious charges to that rap sheet... Abby?" He said, pronouncing the name as if he were addressing a toddler.

She dragged him behind her. "Sorry, officers, we'll make sure he stays in from now on. I hope you have a good day." She gave them as genuine a smile as she could muster.

The officer tipped his cap to her like an old-time cowboy. "You too, miss."

Again, the cop shot her that sarcastic drawl. Ila shut the door quickly but was careful not to slam it in their faces.

Abdul stood breathing heavily, his hands clenched by his side, his tall frame rigid with anger.

Their mother stalked down the hallway. "Abdul Abara! You get changed right now for school..."

But before she could even reach them Abdul had thrown open his bedroom door and slammed it shut.

She and her mother stood with their faces at his door for a moment but her mother seemed resigned to her son's silent dismissal. She beckoned the twins to her and led them from the house.

Ila caught her father's eye as she headed out. His defeated gaze taking in the scene. "Bye, Dad," she offered gently.

In return, the corners of his mouth curled ever so slightly as he attempted to give her a smile.

She hefted her training bag, adjusted her work shirt, and shut the door.

*

His daughter offered him that hopeful smile again. But he couldn't return it. Amir's love for her was as strong as the day he first held her. Now an unnameable pain was smothering it. He picked at the cold, jam-smothered toast before him. The house was now silent, and he listened for the movement of his eldest son. He must talk to the boy. He wanted to guide him. But he no longer knew how.

When Amir had been a boy, any indiscretion or deviation from his father's wishes, or such acts that brought the outside law down on the family, would be punished. He'd lost count of the beatings his father had dished out to he and his brothers. Amir had never wanted to be that sort of parent. He believed in discipline, not brutality. He'd seen enough of that for one lifetime.

The violence had followed him all the way to Australia. He saw it every day in memories like scenes from a film, so clear and real. The memories of he and Rita's homeland played on a constant loop.

He had to force himself to think of the happy times before

the wars. But those scenes were becoming scratchy and faded, just like the old black and white films he sometimes watched on the television.

You must talk to the boy. The police see him more than you do!

Amir forced himself from the kitchen chair and headed toward Abdul's room, moving fast before his slim courage disappeared.

He had to try and understand his son. Did the policeman say he'd been out drinking? Amir hadn't even realised his son wasn't home! He chastised himself; he must do something before his eldest boy was lost to him.

Be firm, but try to understand things are different in this country.

He raised his hand to knock on Abdul's door. A deafening blast of music began pumping from within the room. Instantly Amir's courage deserted him. He couldn't do it. He leant against the wall drained and defeated before he'd even spoken to his son. This was beyond him now and he knew it. Abdul was drifting away and he couldn't even speak to him. *You must try!*

He dropped his hand to his side and wandered back to the kitchen table and his uneaten toast.

CHAPTER 2

Hard eyes scanned the playground, fixing on the group of girls sitting opposite. They were from Rose's year, and were grouped tightly together, legs crossed, hands covering their mouths with all eyes staring back at her.

Rose's jaw twitched and her hands clenched. She'd spent the morning supressing her growing anger but couldn't hold out anymore.

Tierney, the platinum-blonde bombshell, was the girl every boy hungered over. She sat in the midst of her minions like a queen at court. Rose was certain that Tierney had been the one who'd turned all of Year Twelve on her.

Well, all the girls at least.

And here the girl sat, right in front of Rose and talking shit about her. Did she think she could get away with that?

I'm going to fucking shut her up.

Talk shit? Get hit. Wasn't that the old saying?

Rose lent back on the bench and fixed Tierney in her sights. She was going to smash the slut. Rose didn't care about the outcome, so long as she got a few shots on the 'queen'.

A part of her knew she should walk away – it wasn't worth it. It was the last year of school anyway. Who cared what those bitches thought? But the rage grew and Rose channelled it all at the queen with the platinum hair and the fake tan who just sat there spreading lies and making Rose's life at school a misery.

"Where the fuck have you been?" a mouthy voice blurted from behind her. "I've been texting you for ages!"

Rose muttered a greeting as Petra plonked down beside her. Face buried in her phone, and long dark hair covering her eyes, Petra had been her friend since the first day of high school.

Petra came from a huge Turkish family where it was completely natural to yell rather than speak. Rose had to admit, she often felt like a block standing next to the petite, Turkish beauty. *"Looks like a princess, speaks like a tradie,"* was one way their home group teacher had described Petra.

Petra bit down on a huge sausage roll, and yet she could still yell while chewing. Rose was impressed. But all her attention was now locked on the enemy across the way.

"Hey, did you know Amy is having a party?" Petra boomed next to her. "And she didn't even invite me! Bitch! I only found out because Erin is going. Oh my God! You should come too. Just come over to mine to get a drink on first, and we'll walk over…"

Rose was on her feet, stalking across the quadrangle toward the queen and her loyalists.

"Where the fuck are you going?" Petra protested.

Rose flashed her friend a wink and quickened her pace. Petra frowned at her, then looked to where Rose was heading. Rolling her eyes, she stuffed the rest of the sausage roll into her mouth.

She was almost upon the group. Some of the kids in the playground were nudging each other and pointing. They knew something was about to go down.

Rose intended to give them a good show. This would send a strong message to anyone else who wanted to test her.

Tierney spotted her, brushed her hair behind her ear gracefully and stood, arms folded, head tilted in contempt of this peasant that dare approach. As Rose closed the gap, the minions stood to be with their queen.

Tierney raised a perfectly arched eyebrow. "You got a fucken problem, Tanner?"

Without a word, Rose launched at Tierney. The pair crashed to the ground with a resounding smack. Quickly, Rose pulled herself on top of the girl and brought down a series of punishing blows.

The other kids gathered. Phones were out and recording faster than the first punches landed.

Tierney screamed and scratched at Rose in defence. Rose landed a sickening and awkward strike across the bridge of the queen's nose. Blood gushed and Tierney went silent as her eyes rolled back in her head.

For a heartbeat, Rose saw through the red mist engulfing her mind. She glared down at her nemesis. Tierney still looked perfect, her hair had fallen around her in a swirling pattern of white gold. Caught in the midday sun, radiant and shimmering. Even the girl's uniform was still spotless. However, blood flowed freely from her nose, bright and thick. And just for a moment, Rose realised she had wounded her enemy beyond anything she'd intended.

"You fucking psycho," one of Tierney's friends, screamed as she delivered a flurry of open-handed strikes.

The others dived on her, and the red mist fell again. She kicked and punched but there were too many of them.

A blur of dark hair entered the scene as Petra leapt on the back of one of Rose's attackers. Her friend ripped at the girl, riding her like she was in a rodeo.

"Hey! Break it up! All of you!" Rose recognised the voice of Mr Thomas, the Year Nine math teacher.

Gripping her wrist, he yanked her to her feet. "Tanner?" He looked her up and down, then his eyes fell on the groggy and bloody face of the queen. "What the hell is wrong with you?" he demanded, dragging her toward the principal's office.

*

Petra moaned dramatically as Mrs Dover, the school's draconian principal slapped an ice pack into her hand and pressed it against the growing bruise on Petra's cheek. The girl cursed in Turkish, and the principal clipped her over the back of the head.

Mrs Dover peered at them over thick-rimmed glasses. Standing only five feet tall, and slight of build, she was still the most feared educator at their school. Not simply because she was the principal. No, it was that withering gaze she could hold anyone in – child, parent, or another teacher – that instantly caused them to feel inferior.

A simple look from Mrs Dover could do as much damage as a bullet. Rose was certain this skill had taken years to hone, and never failed to be impressed by it, even when she was on the receiving end.

"Back to class, Petra. I'll see you for detention after school," she said grimly.

"Miss! I need to go home, my jaw is broken." Petra always had to get the last word in.

Mrs Dover's eyes were steadfast. "It will be if you don't get out of my office right now."

"Miss? Did you just threaten me?" Petra's hand went to her chest in feigned shock. "My uncle is a lawyer, and if I have to get him down here to defend my human rights—"

"Out!" The older woman's voice hit like a slap. In a flash, Petra snatched up her bag, and was out the door without another word.

Rose let out a stifled chuckle as her friend slipped from the room.

"You think this is funny, do you?"

Rose dropped back into her usual brooding glare. Mrs Dover went behind her desk, pulled out a pink slip of paper and began to write.

"I've just been on the phone to Tierney's parents, they're going to have you charged. You did a nasty number on her, Tanner."

"She was giving me shit! They all were!"

"So you think the solution is to go and put them in hospital?"

Rose swallowed. She didn't know she'd hurt the queen that bad.

"I've told you before, come to me when they do that. Don't go hitting people." Mrs Dover rubbed her forehead and gave a defeated sigh. "Bit late now, isn't it?"

She handed the paper to Rose. "Given the on-going issues we've had with you this year, I have no option but to expel you for now. Your dad's coming to pick you up."

The mention of her father sent an instant whip of anxiety through her. He would be pissed at being woken up, and the police would be heading over to see her too. Her dad hated cops with a passion. And she'd brought them to his house.

"Fuck…" she breathed.

"Indeed," said Mrs Dover. She waved Rose away. "Go on! I'm done with you."

Rose did as she was told.

*

The rumble of her dad's rusted Datsun could be heard well before she saw it. The vehicle crunched to a stop at the school gate. It was difficult to read where her dad's head was at when she got in trouble. Sometimes he'd just want to know if she'd won the fight or not. Other times, he'd maybe give her a slap or just yell. There were times when it seemed he didn't care at all.

Slipping into the passenger seat, she handed him the pink slip. Which reaction would she get? She held her breath and looked him over warily. Rose had inherited her father's height, but that was where their physical similarities ended.

He was tall, fat around the middle from the endless beers and bourbons, with thinning brown hair. Rose was slim, with darker hair, just like her mum's had been. He was her dad, but after her mother had died, he'd stopped being her father. Or rather, given up the job.

He had a new partner now, and they had a daughter together. But he showed no interest in her half-sister, and sometimes even less in his partner.

As much as she hated to admit it, there was one trait they shared.

Anger.

Both had a rage that would erupt like a volcano. It was bubbling right now. The eruption was coming.

His fist whipped out cracking her savagely across the cheek. He coiled it back like a snake ready to strike again.

Rose instinctively raised her hands to defend the strike. He grunted and snatched both her wrists, yanking them down to put his red face inches from hers.

"Don't raise your fucking hands to me," he blustered.

Shoving her against the door, he grinded the gears and drove off.

*

The Datsun grumbled to a stop in front of their Housing Commission unit. Her cheek still ached from the strike, but Rose wouldn't give her dad any satisfaction by crying, or even touching the darkening spot.

She was beyond crying now anyway. He was out of the car and stalking toward the house without a word. Rose hurried to follow.

Entering the unit, a strange flash of nostalgia hit her. For the briefest of moments, she thought her mother was standing there. She'd been young when her mum had passed away, but she remembered the fights her parents used to have, and by the time she was five, Rose knew the drill.

Her dad would come home drunk. Her mum would be at home, also drunk. They'd fight. Rose would hide under her bed, and then either he'd storm off or her mum would storm off, or the cops would come and take him away or her mum away. It was always one or the other.

She'd always hoped that when the cops would take her dad, he wouldn't return. But he always came back.

He's a fucking boomerang, she mused to herself.

Then he'd hit them both. Not with his fists, with his smooth words and gentle touches.

It sounded horrible, but as sad as her mother's death was, at least she wouldn't have to put up with that endless cycle of shit anymore. But she'd been trying to find a happy side in her misery. His anger grew, and now he added his depression on top of it, which he liked to treat with booze and more booze.

The moment they entered the house, he headed straight to the kitchen.

He was going for a drink. She wondered how many he'd sunk that morning.

"What happened, love?" A sweet, sing-song voice caught her attention, and Rose looked up to see Jo seated on the floor with Bethany, her step-sister.

"Got herself in another fucking fix," her dad bellowed as he strutted back into the room, Woodstock and coke in hand. "This time it's for good though."

Bethany charged toward her, an excited smile spreading across her face, her long blonde hair bouncing as she ran.

Rose caught the child in a tight embrace. The kid's smile was infectious; she was only five, and while she smiled a lot, she barely spoke. Beth's teachers believed the little girl could be on the Autism spectrum. But neither Jo nor her dad would get any proper tests done.

Both not only hated cops, but also distrusted authority of any kind. Rose could understand the whole cop thing. After all, she didn't exactly have a glowing relationship with the pigs in blue either. Not many people around their suburb did for that matter. She'd lost count of the number of times she'd been picked up for fighting or smoking weed. Drinking wasn't really her thing. After a lifetime of watching her parents ruin themselves on the stuff, Rose didn't have much inclination for it.

Having said that, she could go a Cruiser right about now. Beth jumped up and down, holding one of her toys out to Rose – a wind-up car that for some reason, her sister was just fascinated with.

"Did it break again?" Rose asked gently.

The child just held it out. Plucking it from the kid's hand, Rose fiddled with the wind-up mechanism. It was pretty old, and often came loose.

Her dad had slurped the last of his drink and crushed the can in his chunky hand. Instantly, he headed back into the kitchen for another.

Jo pursed her lips. "Love, do you have to have another right now?"

"You fucking kidding? I've been dealing with her shit all morning. Think I've earned a few."

Jo's silence marked her acquiescence. She simply nodded and busied herself with tidying the coffee table.

Rose handed the car back to Beth. "Try it now." The child beamed at her, turned the key on the side of the car, placed it on the ground and watched in awe as it raced across the carpet and smacked into the couch.

Returning from the kitchen with another Woodstock, her dad plunked himself on his chair.

"You hungry, love?" Jo asked brightly. "I've got some leftovers if—"

"See!" Her dad lurched to his feet. "That's the bloody problem, Jo. You baby this girl like she's Beth's bloody age! She's eighteen! If she wants food let her sort it out!" He took a hefty swig. "About bloody time you started doing something to earn your keep. Christ knows I've got enough on without having to baby you."

"If drinking was a job, you'd have plenty on," Rose muttered.

The Woodstock can flew across the room. He was on her before she could even register what had happened. Slamming her against the wall, Rose let out a squeal of pain, and her father's hands clamped around her throat.

Beth burst into tears, clutching at her head and shaking. Jo was on her feet begging him to calm down but he silenced her with just one hate-fuelled glare. Jo scooped Beth into her arms.

"You got something to say to me?" he growled. Rose shook her head, tensing her body for another blow.

His voice was soft, almost inaudible. "Don't fucking test me." He released her and headed back to the fridge for yet another Woodstock.

In the following silence, Jo left her daughter and retrieved a mop. She began to wipe up the sticky mix of bourbon and coke from the carpet.

Rose reached out to take the mop. "Let me do it, Jo."

"No, love, I got it. Why don't you take Beth down to the park?"

Rose stood in guilt for a moment watching her step-mum clean. Taking Beth's hand, she walked the sobbing child outside.

CHAPTER 3

Ila sat in the gym's locker room playing with the tattered ends of her belt. She tried to focus on training, but Abdul owned her thoughts. He had all day. A lot of the young guys, in the community got caught up in the so-called, 'Thug Life', but she hadn't thought Abby would get in so deep, and so quickly.

Only the other night she'd overheard him chatting on FaceTime to a couple of his friends, about jumping a kid at school. They'd chatted about bashing someone like they chatted about playing soccer or basketball. Something within her brother had changed, and it scared her.

She snatched her phone from her bag and texted. 'Where were you last night?'

Her feet tapped a busy rhythm on the locker room floor as she waited.

'Out.' Came the reply.

'Did you go to school?'

'Nup,' he shot back. He was being annoyingly dismissive.

'Was dad angry?'

A shrug emoji was her answer.

She pondered for a moment as the thud of body's hitting the mats in the gym resounded. Chewing her bottom lip, she wondered how to get an actual answer out of him? Maybe the direct approach?

'You ok? You've been out a lot this week.'

'See you at home...*mum.*'

She thought about responding but tossed her phone back into her gym bag. Abby used to hang off her every word and listen to her with wide eyes. Now, he was just a pretentious little shit.

Rubbing her weary eyes, she pushed all thoughts of her brother aside for the moment and made a mental note of everything she had to do after training that night. Law essay. Wash her work uniform. Help her mum make the twins' lunches—

The knock on the change room door woke her up. She'd drifted off!

"You decent in there?" her Sensei's voice called.

"Um, yes sorry! I'm coming up now." She started tying her belt around her Gi.

Her Sensai, Michael, stuck his head around the door. He gave her a warm smile. "You all good?"

"Yeah, sorry. Just got caught up with something."

He looked at her thoughtfully for a second. "Could you do me a favour?"

*

Seven years she'd walked the short route from the change rooms to the mats, but she still got nervous heading into training. No matter how much she improved or how many hours she spent on the mats, walking to the Dojo floor filled her with apprehension.

She'd voiced her fears to Michael once, in the hope that he had some pearls of wisdom that would make them disappear.

"Yeah, me too," was all he'd replied with. His dismissive words left her stumped.

How could a Brazilian Jiu Jitsu black belt with fourteen years' experience still get nervous walking into training? In his own Dojo no less!

Michael didn't look like a three-time Pan Pacific and Australian champion. If someone spotted him on the street, they would've probably picked him as an accountant or car dealer. But that was the power of Brazilian Jiu Jitsu, 'The gentle art', as it was called, could give even the smallest of practitioners the ability to dismantle the biggest opponents.

The class was in full swing. There were a few blue belts and brown belts, and only one other purple belt. All were paired up and in the middle of a sparring session, or 'Rolling', as it was commonly called in Jiu Jitsu.

Michael nodded to the middle of the mats. "See that big bloke?"

In the centre of the mats, a rather bulky blue belt was rag-dolling a much smaller blue belt.

Ila observed the burly guy pin the kid to the mats, leap up dropping one knee on the kid's stomach and the other planted on the ground. He then crossed his hands, grabbed either side of the poor kids collar of his Gi and pulled. This was a cross-collar choke, and it was brutally effective. The kid frantically slapped his hand on the mat.

He was tapping out, and when someone tapped out, whether in training or competition, you released them.

The big man smiled, holding the choke for a few seconds longer before finally releasing his beaten opponent.

He bellowed a laugh, slapping the spluttering kid on the back just a tad too hard.

Michael leant in close. "Would you take that bloke down a few pegs? He's new, trained at another place across town. Needs a lesson in humility."

She smiled and headed toward them. Ila was more than happy to bring the big fella back to Earth.

"Hey," she called with an innocent grin. He looked up at her. "Good work on the cross collar. Can we roll for a round?"

He shrugged and hopped up; the kid stepped back to watch. They slapped hands, and bumped knuckles. This was a way of saying that they both agreed to be fair and play by the rules.

He hit her knuckles hard though, almost like a punch. She grinned; he was asking for it.

He grabbed her collar, ready to sweep her to the ground but Ila slipped low, and pushed her backside into his stomach, wrapped her arm around his in one fluid movement and tossed him over her hip to land with a thump on the mat.

Keeping hold of his sleeve, she stepped over his head, flopped on her back and yanked the arm back while pushing her hips against his elbow.

Armbar.

He desperately tapped out.

The kid he'd been roughing around before gasped and smiled as he watched. She gave him a wink.

For the remainder of the round, Ila unloaded on the big blue belt. She swept him to the mat over and again, unleashing her full arsenal. Twisting arms, applying chokes, and catching his legs in foot locks.

He continually tapped out.

She spotted Michael grinning at the scene. But as the round ended, Ila felt the drive to continue. To not just beat this bully, but to utterly flatten him.

The end of the round sounded just as she managed to straddle the man's back, she slipped her right arm quickly under his throat, gripped her left bicep, reached to her shoulder and squeezed.

The rear naked choke.

This was one of the worst techniques to be caught in. You either tapped out or you passed out.

He tapped and tapped but she squeezed tighter and tighter.

Michael's grin faded as the big guy withered in her crushing choke.

Even the kid, who'd been watching his tormentors down fall with glee, was looking on with growing concern.

Finally, she released him. He gazed at her in disbelief, hand to his throat, and his face a red flush.

"Thanks for the warm-up," she muttered nastily. The big fella nodded and moved off the mat slowly.

Rubbing the bridge of his nose, Michael shook his head at her. "All right guys, pair up, let's work some escape drills!"

*

It had been a good session, exactly what Ila needed. Yet her thoughts turned back to her brother. She'd enjoyed her escape into the technical combat of Jiu Jitsu, but it always seemed her anxieties were just waiting to be collected on the way out.

Michael slipped down on the mats in front of her. As her coach for the last seven years, she'd spent more time with him than some of her own family. A connection had developed between them, although she was never sure exactly what to call it. Was it born from the fighter-trainer relationship that grew from all those hours spent in the gym? Or maybe it was something else that was growing? Something more intimate perhaps?

She mentally shook her head at the thought. *He's your friend, that's all. Don't act like a smitten schoolgirl for god's sake.*

He sat before her, still in his full Gi, and raised an eyebrow.

"What?" she asked flatly.

"Went a bit hard, didn't you?"

She shrugged. "The guy's a knuckle-dragger, a mat-bully. It'll be good for him to learn some humility."

His eyes narrowed; Michael had an annoying ability to pick up her deeper issues. "You want to tell me what's really up?"

"Nothing, just some shit with my brother."

He gave a nod of understanding. "You know you can always bring him here, right? Might be good for him."

"Nah, I don't think this is really his style," she said.

The weight of her brother's issues, her father's depression, and the endless expectations her mother was dumping on her were dragging her down. That chain of responsibility was firmly strapped around her neck. Suddenly he rolled backwards on to the training area.

"I want to work on something with you," he said fixing his Gi and waving her over.

She shuffled out on the mats.

"So," he said, slipping back into coaching mode. "I've noticed you've been struggling to sweep the big guys from guard. Give it a shot."

Ila flopped onto her back, and he knelt before her while she wrapped her legs around his waist.

"Now try and sweep me," he said.

She planted her left foot on the ground, dragged him toward her, and swept her right leg under his arm.

He was unmoved, a sly grin on his face. "Come on Ila, this is white belt stuff. Get your right leg right under my arm. Be explosive."

A huff of frustration escaped her. She whipped her right leg up and dragged him down.

A gasp of surprise escaped him as he was flung on his back. Now she was astride him in the 'mount' position. The intimacy of the position was not lost on either of them.

"Better?" he stammered.

"Feels very… powerful," she said with a coy smile.

The moment seemed to last forever. She could feel the

tension between them. Or maybe he was just waiting for her to get the hell off him. But his eyes hovered on her. Neither of them was making the move to break the position.

Finally, he broke the moment. "Nice job. We need to start working on that striking too. The Warrior tournament is coming up soon, you still keen?" he said, hopping up.

The image of her mother's disapproving face appeared in her head. She still hadn't told her mother about their plans to enter the amateur fight competition. "I... I don't think I can," she mumbled.

"What? You were dead keen a month ago. I see you watching that promo video for it every time you're in here," he said, trying to hide his disappointment.

"It's just a bit complicated at the moment." She moved toward the change rooms. "I better go, got an assignment due. Thanks for the roll, Mike." She offered a genuine smile, but hurried off without another word, dragging his disappointment with her.

*

The house was strangely still when she got home. Usually, the twins would come stampeding down the hall to greet her as the blare of the television and her brother's music assaulted her ears.

But there was only blissful silence.

Moving through to the kitchen, she dumped her bags and snatched an apple from the fruit bowl. Pulling her reading assignment from the pile of Uni books in her bag, she sat at the kitchen table and read, enjoying the quiet. But it was short lived.

"Yo!" Abdul's voice bellowed from his room.

"Just me!" she called back. "Where's Mum and Dad?"

"They took the twins to swimming or something." He appeared behind her. "You gonna go blind from all that reading, girl."

She smiled thinly up at him. "You're the one who's going to go blind. All that alone time you spend in your room." She mimed wanking, complete with wet sound effects.

He shoved her playfully. "Piss off! What is this shit anyway?" He snatched the book from her and started reading aloud. Holding it up high so she couldn't snatch it back. "The Mabo case was a significant legal case in Australia that recognised the land rights of the traditional owners of the Murray Islands. The Mabo case challenged the existing Australian legal system from two perspectives..." He rolled his eyes at her. "Blah, blah, blah..." He tossed the book back. "What's a Maboo or whatever?"

"Mar-bo," she corrected. "He helped Aboriginal land claims be recognised by law. I'm doing an assignment on him for Uni."

He nodded as he rummaged through the fridge. "So he took on the power? Sounds like a real 'G'."

She flattened the book back on the table. "Yeah, I guess he was."

"Fuck all good it did them. They got it worse than us," he said, stalking out.

But she felt his comment was pointed to her. "What do you mean?" she asked, perhaps a little pointedly herself. But he was already in his room.

Abandoning the book, she went after him. He had a habit of making a combative statement, and then simply walking off on her. Usually, she'd just let it slide but tonight, given all the crap he'd been doing recently, she wouldn't let him get away with speaking to her disparagingly.

Ila threw open his door. "Who's got it worse than us?"

He sniffed. "The Abos."

She gave him an appalled look. "Don't use that fucking word!"

"What? I don't mean it in a bad way. I'm just saying its true!"

She rubbed at her eyes. "What exactly do you mean? Are you saying *we* have it bad?"

He shook his head at her like he was talking to a naive child. As he spoke, he reached under his bed, retrieved a small box, and began to roll a joint. The smell of the dope assaulted her senses.

"Are you that fucking blind, girl?" he said softly. "There's a reason the pigs boost me every week. I mean, *fuck me*, we can't even walk anywhere without getting, 'the look'," he said, complete with air quotes.

It was her turn to roll her eyes. "What look?"

"You know! That fucking nervous sideways look white people give you whenever you walk past."

He made a great show of giving her an over-the-top suspicious glance. This amused him no end. "Man, they shit themselves every time something dark walks by. I'm surprised their own shadows don't scare them!" He laughed, slapping his knee for extra effect. He finished rolling the joint, admiring his creation for a moment.

She sat next to him on the bed. "You don't think it's got anything to do with you and your boys slamming beers in the park at three in the morning? On a school night no less?"

"We weren't hurting anyone! Pigs always act like we out there hustling all the time."

She sniggered. "Hustling?"

Again, he gave her a playful shove. "Shut up, you know what I mean." He laughed.

She looked her brother over as he lit the joint and flopped back on the bed. Ila wasn't blind, and despite what Abdul might think, she wasn't immune to being glared at when she went to the shops or out to eat. She'd lost track of the number of times she'd been followed around a store by security guards, who just always seemed to be in the same aisle as her.

There was a stigma that went along with being Sudanese or even just being black. It didn't matter that she was born in Australia, that she had an Australian accent like her friends.

She was different.

Yet she shook her head defiantly. "They aren't all like that. Just like every African isn't a wanna be thug," she said.

"You're just saying that because you got that buff white boy you roll around with all day." He winked up at her before rolling on his side and twisting his arm behind his back. "Oh, submit me, Michael!" He called in a surprisingly good imitation of her voice. "Submit me!"

She grabbed his arm and twisted his wrist. "Ah! Fuck! Ok,

tap out! I tap out!" Ila released him and he rubbed his wrist. "Fuck, girl, you're getting too good at that Jiu Jitsu shit."

"You should come and train," she said. "You'll love it."

"What? Dress up in pyjamas and roll around on the ground with a bunch of sweaty guys? Don't think so."

He took a long drag on the joint, and then held it out to her.

She shook her head.

"Come on," he teased. "I promise I won't tell Mum her golden girl is a drug addict."

She acquiesced and took the joint taking the lightest of puffs. This was his way of offering peace. Of saying, let's just agree to disagree. But still she couldn't let his assumptions go.

"Do you really believe every white person thinks... you know, like that?"

He grunted in frustration, bolting up suddenly. She was about to get a blast of Abdul's anger. But she stared back, unflinching as he spoke.

"Listen, you can fucking go to law school and be the token African girl for them to put on their advertisement posters or whatever. Hell, you can play at being the next fucking... Marooboo—"

"Mar! Bo!"

"What! Ever!"

She opened her mouth to speak again but he shook his finger in her face.

"Ila! You know what this fucking place is like. You know what they're like. All this shit stays the same and you know it.

So stop fucking kidding yourself."

She handed the joint back and stood to leave. "I have to study."

"You have to wake up."

She thought about a retort, but in the end she simply walked out.

He blew a long puff of smoke after her.

CHAPTER 4

She was pushing her luck, but if Rose could just get past her dad, she could be out of the house before he remembered he was supposed to be furious at her.

He'd been drinking steadily all day but had been on his best behaviour when the cops arrived. In turn, Rose had played the part of the remorseful daughter. The cops simply took a statement, and said they would refer the whole thing to her caseworker. Then the two played the good cop, bad cop routine. It was an actual real tactic they used. Just like in the movies.

One had tried to get her to open up about "...how things were at home." But she wasn't going to put Jo, and herself, through another round with her dad.

Once the cops were gone, her dad had parked himself in front of the tv to watch the footy. His dinner plate balanced on his knees. Thankfully, Collingwood were playing well tonight.

Seeing he was happily docile and munching on his food, she made her move. The party she and Petra were heading to wouldn't have many kids from her school, and definitely none of Tierney's friends would be there.

She made a bee-line for the front door. "See you guys

soon," she said softly.

"Where you going?" he asked without looking up from the game.

"Just over to P's house."

"You think so, do you? After all the shit you put me through today?" He didn't even glance up from the game.

Her hang-dog look returned. It had been worth a try. Then Jo's face popped around from the kitchen. "Let her go, love. It's only around the corner. You don't want her cooped up here all night, do you?"

He finally turned to her. She hated the way his eyes took her in with their disconnected gaze. It was like she was just an object. "You're just going to P's?"

She nodded slowly.

He held his plate out to Jo. "More salt."

Jo took the plate back into the kitchen. His eyes were on her again. Lingering in all the places that made her flesh creep.

She shifted uncomfortably, clutched her bag in front of her. Hoping it obscured his view.

"You worry me, Rosie, you know that?" he said gently. "That's why I get the way I do. I don't want to hurt you... Shit! I don't want to hurt anyone!" He reached out and took her hand. "I'm just trying to do what's best." His thumb rubbed her fingers, rough and sweaty. The softness of his touch sent a repellent shock through her whole body. Gripping her hand tightly, he lent in close. "You're looking more and more like your mother. You know that?"

He gazed up at her. His eyes held a distinct predatory

gleam, and the sickly smell of coke and bourbon wafted from his breath.

Jo returned, and he instantly released her. Only then did she realise that she'd been holding her breath the whole time.

Snatching the plate from Jo, he waved her away with his other hand. "Go on, piss off then, and don't be late."

She and Jo shared a brief look, and her step-mum offered a gentle smile. Rose hurried out as Collingwood kicked another goal.

She hoped the team would hold on to win. She knew what her dad would be like if they lost, especially with a days' worth of drinking under his belt.

CHAPTER 5

Ila's eyes grew heavy, despite the beats pumping through her headphones. The words on her laptop were looking like splotches of ink spilled across a page.

The headphones were carefully taken from her head, and the deep beats slipped away to a tinny drone as her mother laid them down on her desk.

"How's it coming along?" The elder woman swept Ila's long braids from her face. She looked down on her with pride.

Ila rubbed her eyes, stretching back from her desk. "Finished most of it."

Her mother leafed through a few pages. "This is good." She nodded encouragingly.

"I might stop for tonight, my eyes are killing me."

"No, keep going," she said. She was giving her most encouraging look. "Listen Ila, you finish it now and then you'll have more time to polish it up tomorrow."

"Yeah, I know Mum, but I've got training in the morning..."

Her mother's heavily lined face changed instantly, to a questioning frown. "It's not good enough to simply pass. You have to finish at the top to get the best opportunities. You spend too much time on this Karate nonsense—"

"She's doing her best, Rita."

They spun to the droll voice. Her father stood in the doorway, his frame stooped, his brow heavy.

Her mother glowered at him. "If she's going to make anything of herself, she needs to get the best results. That will only happen if she pushes harder than the other students—"

"Look at her," he protested. "She needs rest."

"She can rest when she's finished!"

"You're too hard on her!"

"They have one opportunity!" Her mother brandished her fist at him. "One! She needs to make the most of it, or she'll end up just like us with no future and…" Her mother looked away.

Ila knew what she'd been about to say, and she knew the shame her dad felt. He'd been a man of note back in Sudan. Though they never said exactly what it was he'd worked as, Ila suspected that it was something high up in some sort of local government role.

But the war had taken that from him.

This was a wedge between her parents. The older she got, the more she understood why her mum pushed her so hard to excel at her studies. To rebuild the family's honour.

"It's ok, Dad," she said. "I'm almost done anyway."

He was about to speak when Abdul stamped passed him in the hallway.

Her mother was after him in a flash. "Abdul!"

Ila kept her eyes on the pages as the commotion in the hallway played out.

"I'm just going out for a bit, relax," he moaned.

"Get back inside now," her mother yelled.

"I'll be back later!"

The front door opened and slammed shut. There was a moment of silence before her mother began spraying insults at her dad. Her father muttered back, his voice flat and broken.

Ila slipped her headphones back on, breathing deeply as the heavy beats drowned out her parents' argument.

She pumped the volume and turned her bloodshot eyes back to the assignment. It looked like she would get it done tonight after all. The pressure was all on her now. Ila was painfully aware that she was the last beacon for her parents' hope. Well, in her mother's eyes at least.

CHAPTER 6

H er dark-haired friend danced around her room like no one was watching, as music pounded from the speakers. Rose downed another Cruiser, watching as Petra tossed clothing from her closet on to her bed.

"I got court in a few days," Rose stated.

Petra's response came muffled from inside the closet. "Already?" More clothes flew over her shoulder on to the bed.

"I was on a caution from the last one so…"

"Fuck, Rosie, you gotta stop smashing people."

"You sound like Principal Dover!"

"Hey, I copped a week of after school detentions for jumping in and saving your ass, princess!" Her head popped around the closet door. "You're welcome by the way." Petra held out a floral mini skirt. "Too slutty?"

Rose screwed up her face. Petra shrugged and dove back into her closet.

"You know what those fucking bitches are like," Rose protested.

"Yeah, but you're always punching on. There's hardly anyone in our year you haven't jumped or started shit with."

"I just wanted them to stop talking shit about me."

Petra stepped out from behind her door. "What about all the other times?"

Rose had no response. She sipped at her drink in silence. Petra gazed quizzically.

"What?" Rose asked.

"How's your dad been?"

Rose took a long drink.

"That good huh?"

"Just... don't worry about it. I don't want to think about him tonight."

Petra looked ready to push her on the subject, but instead returned to her clothes. Rose finished her drink, and immediately opened another one.

Petra stepped out from behind the closet door. "What about this."

Rose almost dropped her drink in amazement. Petra had settled on a figure-hugging black number. With her dark hair spilling around her shoulders, and the dress's soft sparkle, she was the embodiment of mature elegance and glamor.

Rose couldn't form the words to express how utterly stunning she looked.

Petra's shoulders slumped as she misread her friend's expression. She was the moody eighteen-year-old again. "Fuck man, I thought this one was ok," Petra said grumpily.

"No... P. You look... awesome."

But Petra was clearly not convinced.

"Seriously," Rose pressed. "It looks perfect on you."

Petra's face lit up. "Come on let's finish these up and get going. One more big night before they put you in the new black." Petra grabbed a drink and began scrolling through her phone. Rose couldn't stop looking her over. It was like she was seeing the wild Turk for the first time.

Something was starting to happen when she was with her friend. Admittedly, she didn't really understand it, and *it* – whatever *it was* – made her feel things that she hadn't before.

"P... I... I um..."

Petra swept her dark locks back as she looked up at her expectantly. Rose felt *it* hit her again.

"Well, I just wanted to... Shit, I don't know... thank you, I think..."

Petra shook her head. "Chill bitch! You're not going to jail—"

"No... I mean, well I know that, what I think I mean is—"

"Rosie, you better not be pulling a D and M on me. I just spent thirty minutes getting this eye make-up smoky as fuck, and if you make me cry and wreck them..."

Rose burst into laughter. Whatever words she was searching for, maybe now was not the time.

Petra closed her phone and finished her drink. "Listen, fuck the courts, and fuck your dad. Don't think about it. Tonight is your night." A mischievous gleam entered her eyes. "I'm going to get you fucked up."

*

They arrived at the party to find it utterly out of control. Petra couldn't be more excited. Grabbing Rose's arm, Petra dragged her through the throng of people on the front lawn and into the house.

Rose spotted a few kids from their school. Most of the other kids were around their age, but there were plenty of crashers who weren't. She recalled it was Amy, a girl in their year, who was throwing the party, but there was no sign of her anywhere. In fact, the more she and Petra made their way around the house, the more it became clear that Amy's party had been well and truly gate-crashed.

"Her folks are gonna kill her," Petra giggled.

Every which way Rose looked, there was booze and drugs on offer.

Eventually they found a group of girls Petra knew in the back yard, and they joined them as the party raged on. But throughout the chaos and the many bottles of Cruisers she downed, Rose's eyes kept falling to Petra.

Every time her friend touched her, or even just laughed at some stupid joke she made, an excited rush whipped through her. It was a nice feeling, but still strange and confusing.

But sometimes, even in the anarchy around them, it felt like she and P were the only two there.

CHAPTER 7

A bdul didn't care what his mum thought, and he definitely didn't give a shit if his Dad was disappointed in him. He just wanted to live for the moment. Long ago, when he stilled bothered with school, he'd realised that the life his parents obsessed over wasn't for him.

Just look at Ila! She was slaving away at work and university. He knew for a fact she hated her job at the supermarket, and was only studying law because their mum had decided on it for her.

Admittedly he *did* care what Ila thought. He didn't like it when she gave him those hurt eyes. It was the way she folded her arms and looked down, then back up at him, like he had attacked everything she believed in. But as clever as she was, the girl was ignorant of the real world. She'd spent too much time with her head in books.

He felt for her, however. After all, she was the one their parents had pinned their hopes on.

The din from the party was growing. He must be getting closer.

Abdul quickened his step.

Two stumbling, drunk boys slipped out of his way as they came from the opposite direction. Abdul had sprung up in the last year. At only seventeen, he was much taller than most. But in the scraps he'd been in, he'd found out quickly that it didn't really mean much.

His phone buzzed. It was a message from his school mate, Marley: 'How far off man?'

He texted back: 'Almost there.'

Marley shot back the middle finger emoji. 'Meet you at the front.'

Abdul rounded the corner of the street and spotted the house. Nodding his approval with an excited smile, he headed in. The party was pure ruckus! There were people everywhere. This was going to be awesome!

Marley and the others were gathered on the huge front porch of the house. Beers and joints being passed back and forward. They all let out a cheer when they spotted him. Before he'd even shook hands with all of them, he had Vodka in one hand and a joint hanging from his mouth.

They sat for a while on the porch watching the talent come and go.

"Bro, there's a fucking smorgasbord tonight," Marley said, rubbing his hands together.

"Keep it in your pants," Abdul said between tokes. "You start flashing that whale around, they'll all faint."

A howl of laughter ripped through his friends. But then Abdul spotted a car creeping passed the front of the house.

The headlights were on low, and the music emanating from

within went suddenly silent. Five or six outlines of heads were visible. The red glow of a lit cigarette illuminated the driver for a brief moment.

"Who the fuck is that?" Abdul asked, nodding to the car.

Marley was on his feet in a second, chest puffed and his hands clenched. "It's those Casey boys. Fucking pussies!"

The car stopped in the middle of the street.

Its occupants had spotted them.

Abdul launched himself off the porch. "You want to do something, bitch!"

The driver of the car took another puff on his smoke. The red glow illuminating his face once again and giving his eyes a devilish glow.

The car's gears crunched, and it screeched away from the house. Abdul's boys hooted and yelled after it.

None of them noticed the car pull a U-turn at the end of the street.

CHAPTER 8

Rose held Petra's hair back as she spewed across the pavement. They were leaning on the fence out the front of the house. The party was winding up now, and the early hours of the morning were upon them.

Ride shares were picking up drunken kids. Some had paired off and were spread out on the lawn, but the party had well and truly burned itself out.

She couldn't help but giggle at the whole thing. This was meant to be a small gathering but word had gotten around, and people had come from everywhere. It turned out Amy, the host, had been passed out in her room for the whole night. The house was trashed, and there was no doubt that her parents were going to kill her when they returned.

Petra's bleary, bloodshot eyes looked up at her. "This is your fault! Why did you let me mix drinks?"

"I drank as much as you," Rose said with a laugh. "Not my fault you're soft."

"Stop talking so loudly, my head's killing me. Where's this lift?"

Rose glanced at her phone. "Not too far."

Two tall African boys stepped out on to the porch and

flashed a look at the pair. But then more boys came out and the group started playfully pushing and shoving each other around. They'd clearly pinched booze from someone, and were now passing it between each other.

"Your shoulders are really uncomfortable by the way," Petra grumbled as she flopped back on Rose.

Rose smiled as she brushed the dark locks from Petra's face. She felt that odd feeling come over again as she gazed on her friend. But she pushed the feeling aside, and looked down at her phone. Their ride was closer. A car approached. "I think it's here," she announced.

But why the hell did the car have its headlights off? Suddenly it sped up and came to a screeching halt in front of the house.

Doors flew open and five boys scurried out. They cleared the fence, and sprinted across the lawn.

One of the African boys yelled a warning. The group on the porch turned, spotted the others and jumped down to engage them.

The two sides crashed together. Fists and kicks flew. Rose dragged Petra away from the chaos, and onto the street.

"Tell them to shut up? I've got a fucking headache," Petra mumbled.

It was a nasty fight. The moment someone went to the ground, they were kicked and stomped on until their group jumped the other group.

Rose watched the brawl with a sort of grim interest. Both sides were tiring now, but the damage was done. Three boys lay unconscious yet fists were still flying.

She spotted their ride and waved it down, sliding into the back seat with Petra.

"Everything ok?" the driver asked fearfully.

"Yeah, just another fuck or fight Friday," she mumbled back.

*

After depositing Petra at her front door, she gave her a prolonged hug, which Rose had thought was sweet. Then she realised Petra had fallen asleep. She'd got her inside then walked back around the corner to home.

The sun was peaking over the buildings as she carefully unlocked the screen door, then the heavy front door. The house was silent and dark. Her dad wouldn't be up until at least midday, given the number of cans of Woodstock strewn next to the couch.

She stood for a moment in the living room and became aware of how drunk she was herself.

She flopped on the couch as the world went black.

*

Rose woke to a cold hand on her leg. Her chest tightened and she squeezed her eyes closed.

Don't move. No matter what, just don't move.

"Rosie, you awake?" a gravel voice whispered.

It was her dad.

She was lying facing away from him. This at least made it easier to feign sleep. He'd done this before but he usually left her alone if she didn't move. And never had it gone any further then touching. But she didn't want to find out if he *would* try and take it another step further.

Do. Not. Move.

His hand slid up to her backside. It lingered there. She cringed.

"Just like your mother," he whispered.

Holding her breath, she tried to keep still as possible. Now his hand was stroking her back. Rose desperately tried not to flinch away. If she did, he'd know she was awake. Holding herself still, she hoped he would just leave her alone.

Suddenly his hand whipped away, and he jerked to standing.

Soft feet padded toward her. A blanket was thrown over her body. Her father grunted his frustration and hurried from the room.

Cautiously she shifted her body, still pretending to be asleep. Opening her eyes slightly, she spotted Beth sitting on the floor in her pyjamas, playing with the wind-up toy.

Rose reached her hand out to her sister. Beth took it and smiled brightly.

CHAPTER 9

Flicking stinging sweat from her eyes she reset into her fighting stance. Left foot forward, right foot back. Her weight balanced, breathing steady.

The gym was a furnace tonight, and she knew Michael loved it like that. Both were in rash guard and shorts. Her hands covered by twelve-ounce gloves, her shins protected by guards, and with her braids tied up and spilling down her back, Michael had jokingly called her, "The Predator."

All around them the sound of shins cracking off kick pads and heavy breathing filled the dense air.

"Do the combo again!" he ordered. "Remember, timing over power!"

He raised the focus pads.

Ila stalked forward. Left jab, straight right, left roundhouse kick.

She threw the combination over and over as they moved around the mats. Her legs and core screamed as the lactic acid built, but Michael drove her on, pushing her to work through the pain.

"The longer you go, the stronger you get!" he yelled.

She stepped back and without thinking dropped her hands

from protecting her chin. He gave her cheek a playful slap with the pads. "Hands up, Predator, don't get lazy."

Mercifully, the timer dinged to end the round. She dropped to her knees, breathing deeply, heart still pounding.

Michael, as always, looked calm and relaxed. He grinned, enjoying her struggle.

"Can we open a window at least," she begged.

His grin widened and he shook his head slowly.

She struggled to her feet, legs quivering like a newborn foal.

"You're doing well," he said. "You just gotta stay consistent."

"I won't be able to stand up with those girls. They're too strong. And all will be better strikers."

"So what? Take the fight to the ground, that's where you're strong. Fight on your terms not theirs." He ripped off the focus pads and tossed them aside. He threw her a pair of MMA gloves and slipped some on himself. "Let's try the combo, but this time add the take down."

She looked at him uncertainly.

"Come on, Ila, you're not a purple belt because the colour brings out your eyes."

She cracked her knuckles and bounced forward, as the timer sounded the start of a new round.

They sparred lightly, throwing punches and kicks but with minimal impact. He nodded approval as she blocked his attack and countered. "Good, now throw the combo and go for the take down. Let's work!"

She hopped forward, lightly balanced on both feet.

Left jab, straight right, left round house, then she dropped to one knee, slipped to the side, caught his leg, lifted it and drove him back into the floor.

She slipped up in to mount position, and threw down punch after punch.

"Good!" he called as he defended, now go for the submission!"

Ila wrapped her arm around his neck, switched her position to the side. His other arm was caught over his head.

She squeezed down, and he tapped out almost immediately as the breath was driven from his throat.

She rolled away while he lay panting on his back. "Arm triangle," he said with a satisfied grin. "Brutal."

She helped him to his feet.

"You see? Their stand-up game won't mean shit once you take it to the ground. Got it, Predator?"

She gave an exaggerated bow. "Yes, Sensei!"

Michael stepped forward and kicked her legs out from under her. She landed in a heap with a groan of pain. "Remember though, they can do the same to you."

She struggled up to her elbows and blew her braids out of her face.

"Now get up! One more round before we finish. You want to win the Warrior comp? You got to work harder than everyone else."

"Trust me," she said. "I am."

The gym's small parking lot was baking in the midday sun. Ila smiled up at the burning ball of fire, enjoying the heat on her skin. Melbourne was so often draped in wind and rain that you had to take these opportunities to soak up some rays when it came.

Michael emerged from the two-storey building, his training bag slung over his shoulder. "You want to grab something to eat?" he asked, a slight nervousness in his voice. "If you haven't got anything on, I mean, and just to go over training and all that sort of stuff."

She hid her knowing smile. "I can't. Gotta get back to work."

"Busy girl."

"Told you I was working hard."

"Never doubted it." He shifted his bag, locking his eyes on her and dropping back into coach mode. "So, I can get you a fight in the amateurs pretty soon. We need to start getting serious about—"

"Listen, Mike. I just need a bit more time. My mum's still not on board—"

"Then what are we doing here?" His disappointment was palpable. "The Warrior comp isn't that far off."

She wanted so badly to throw herself into the training. She wanted to be a fighter more than anything. Certainly, she wanted it more than becoming a lawyer. Her mother's burning eyes flashed in her mind. Jesus, it was almost like her mum was there right now.

"Listen," he said dropping his bag and fixing her with a stern gaze. "I've been doing this for a long time. I know when someone is ready to take that next step to serious competition, but you must be all in. You can't just, sort of want to do it."

"I understand that!" she said desperately. "But my mum… she… she just wants me to do well. I have to perform at Uni—"

"You don't think other fighters are the same?" he said, gesturing to the gym. "Not one of those fighters work any less hard than you, or have any easier decisions to make."

"But my mum—"

"Won't let you?"

She fell silent.

His gaze softened slightly. "Ila, this is your life. Your choice."

"It's not that simple!"

He nodded snatching up his bag. "If you want to do this, then I'm here to go on the journey with you. But if not, then let me know quickly so I can start focusing on those that do."

He strode to his car before she could say another word.

CHAPTER 10

The courthouse felt like a second home, and that wasn't a good thing. Rose sat in the same waiting area she'd sat last time... and the time before that. Her dad wasn't interested in coming down with her anymore. He was usually too hungover anyway.

At least Jo had come with her. But her step-mum looked fatigued, her eyes heavy and dark ringed. She gripped Rose's hand as people bustled around them. Beth was with them of course. Sitting on her mum's lap, legs kicking excitedly, she watched the people pass with awe-filled eyes.

A sudden stab of regret hit Rose. This was no place for a little girl. Nor was it anything Jo needed to deal with. God knew Jo had enough on her plate with her dad, looking after Beth, and now having to chaperone her to court.

If the court gave her a... what did they call it? Custodial sentence? Maybe it would be good for Jo and Beth if Rose wasn't around for a bit. But did she trust her dad to be left alone with them? She scratched at her fringe, squeezed her eyes tight with frustration.

What could she do to protect them from him? She couldn't

even protect herself.

"Jo, isn't it?"

They all wheeled around to the officious voice.

A lithe man in a tight suit appeared, a stack of files hugged to his chest. He grabbed Jo's hand and shook it.

"I'm David, if you remember," he said. Jo opened her mouth to speak, but he was already pulling Rose to her feet. He was dark haired and tall, always looking like he'd just rolled out of bed, and yet he somehow made it work.

"Come on, Rose, we're about to start. Here we go again, hey?" he laughed.

David had taken over as her caseworker a few months ago. Unlike all the other caseworkers and lawyers who had represented her, it felt like he was truly on her side. He was always working hard to get her the best outcome, and she knew she was lucky. Many other caseworkers and lawyers seemed frankly burned out and checked out.

Leading them down a busy corridor, he spoke as if he were pinging on speed. His voice rapid, but clear. "I've managed to pull a few strings to get you a work placement. Had to call in a favour so please behave!"

Jo opened her mouth again to speak, but David was only pausing for breath. "I'm going to be up front with you here, it's not going to be a holiday, but it's certainly a step up from the other option."

"Which is?" Jo asked, finally getting a word in. *Two* words in.

"Detention; and not the kind they give you in school."

They finally arrived at a door marked, Court C. "Just stay quiet unless she addresses you directly."

David opened the door, and ushered them in. The room looked more like a meeting room in an office than a court of law. All white walls and grey desks. People sat writing notes and typing on computers.

Rose felt like she was just one part of some massive machine, which was about to either swallow her whole or spit her out in disgust.

Jo hushed Beth as they sat.

The child half calling out to Rose as David led her to the front. Another case was being heard. Some tall African kid was standing before the magistrate and looking like he was actually rather bored with the whole situation. Rose thought he looked slightly familiar. Was he the one at that party last week?

The judge was giving her final decision. You could sometimes pick up on the magistrate's mood by how they treated the poor kid who was up before you.

"…Abdul Abara, I accept your guilty plea. I will take into account your counsel's argument that you did not initiate the fight. I'm therefore placing you on a good behaviour bond, and fifty hours community service."

"Thank you, your honour," his lawyer said, and ushered the boy out, as if he was worried she might change her mind.

"All right, let's keep this moving," the magistrate said, barely stifling a yawn.

David directed Rose to the front, and she stood feeling very self-conscious, as the magistrate went over her notes. The woman put on a pair of glasses that magnified her eyes, then proceeded to glare down at Rose.

The glasses gave the magistrate the appearance of an owl looking down on a captured mouse. Rose really did feel small standing before her now.

"Ah, Miss Tanner. Back again, are we?" Rose said nothing. She must've had this woman before but she couldn't remember when. The judge continued to flick through the files before her. "I must say, Miss Tanner, this is quite the record you're building here." The magistrate turned those big owl-eyes to David. "Does your client have a plea?"

He stood. "Yes your honour, guilty."

The magistrate scribbled some more notes. Someone in the room yawned.

"Now, Miss Tanner," she continued. "Given your previous record, my first thought is to give you a custodial sentence."

Rose's breath left her. She'd let her temper get the better of her one too many times, and now it was catching up with her.

"However..." The owl was speaking again. "I'm of the understanding that your counsel has an option to present?"

David nodded. "Yes your honour. I've been in contact with a youth placement program that I think Rose would benefit from. It hasn't been used in a while—"

"Where?"

He pulled a page from his files and handed it to the judicial officer who passed it along.

The magistrate read the page then grinned cruelly down on Rose. "I didn't know that place was still running. Very well,

I actually think this could work. Miss Tanner, do you have anything you'd like to say?"

Rose's voice left her for a moment. "N-no."

The magistrate glared at her.

"Your honour," Rose said quickly. "No, your honour."

A pleased smile stretched across the magistrate's lips. "I'm sentencing you to two hundred hours in the program."

She quickly ripped off her glasses. Her flat stare froze Rose's heart mid-beat.

"Let me make one thing crystal clear, Miss Tanner. This is absolutely your final opportunity.

If you appear before this court again, or you do not complete your placement, I will have no hesitation in sentencing you to the maximum term of incarceration. Is that quite clear?"

Rose felt faint. "Y-yes, your honour."

CHAPTER 11

I t had been a week since the party, and Abdul had to admit, he'd copped some solid hits. He still had a slight headache from the fight.

His size made him a target despite him hoping it would work the other way. Most of the time people just got out of his way and left him alone. He thought it was funny the way people shifted awkwardly when he sat next to them on the train. Or the way they'd quicken their step if he walked behind them on the street.

He stepped across the road toward the soccer ground. Sitting on benches on the far side, his boys were waiting. A cheer rose from the group when they spotted him. He flashed them the finger back, with a toothy smile.

It was going to be another good night. But the throbbing in his head was a reminder that he better make sure it was a quiet one. The Casey boys had gotten some good shots in. He knew why they'd targeted him. Everyone wants a rep, and the best way to get it? Knock out the biggest guy on the other team.

Marley tossed him a can of Bourbon. "How'd it go, man?"

He shrugged. "Same shit."

"You got community?" Marley asked.

"Hey, it was fucking worth it! Give those pricks some smoke."

They all cheered again. As they chatted, Abdul took them all in. Most of them had records, or at least a few issues with the pigs. The way some of them looked at him, it messed with him a bit. Like they were always expecting him to be the hardest, and the one that wouldn't back down. It worried him. He had a reputation, and it was hard to shake. If there was a fight, they expected him to be straight in. If they were drinking, everyone assumed he would go hard and long into the night.

He couldn't be that guy forever, could he?

Ila slipped into his thoughts. She was making something of herself. He had to give her credit. She forever had her head buried in the books, which couldn't be easy with Mum peering over her shoulder at every single thing she did.

But that wasn't him. He was never going to be a Uni graduate.

His hand clenched at his side. The grievance he felt at this fucking world, at himself, was souring his mood fast. He suddenly wished the Casey boys would roll up again.

"Bro?"

He clicked out of his thoughts. Marley stood in front of him, eyes quizzical. "You good?"

"Yeah," Abdul said, forcing a smile. He needed to get out of this rut. "I could go a fucking drink session though."

"Yeah, we should do a Bottleshop runner," one of the other boys said.

A thought popped into Abdul's head. Even as he thought it, a vision of Ila at their front door came to him. Her see-all eyes holding him with that deep hurt as the pigs dumped him on their doorstep.

He shouldn't do it. He knew he shouldn't do it.

Fuck it!

He was already walking when Marley called, "Where you off to?"

"I'll be back in a second," he said with a wink.

*

A young couple stepped out of his way as he walked into the store, giving him, 'the look'.

"Getting a bit too dark for you, is it?" he barked.

Their pace increased. Abdul shook his head with a laugh. *They're all the same.* He headed straight for the fridge and stacked his arms with three six packs of Bourbon and coke. Turning to the counter, he made sure to slam the fridge door behind him.

A little Asian lady stared up at him from behind the counter, her arms folded protectively across her chest.

He chuckled in disbelief; this was too easy. "How much for these?"

"Sixty-six dollars," she said.

"Good to know."

He walked out, calm and slow. The lady stood grimly. What could she do? Call the cops? Yell at him to come back and pay?

Abdul spat on the sidewalk and stared down a middle-aged man who was walking past. He laughed in the man's face.

None of them could stop him.

Abdul walked tall and proud. He walked strong.

*

The boys cheered and patted him on the back upon his return. He threw a can to Marley, giving him a wide grin. They drank and laughed.

Abdul brushed off worries of his sister and his future. Nothing mattered but right now. He stood with his boys, staring across the soccer pitch toward the distant city monoliths.

He didn't care if he had a target on his back. Let them come and try.

After all, what could they do? He felt emboldened by this simple realisation.

No one can fuck with me.

Abdul stood a little taller.

CHAPTER 12

Her parents sat, eyes glued to the television, the news from Sudan blazing away on screen. Ila watched from the kitchen table surrounded by her books, trying not to get distracted by the same news stories she always saw.

Poverty. War. Corruption.

Sometimes the order was different. Sometimes the people on the screen were different. But to Ila, it seemed the news was just on a cycle.

Poverty. War. Corruption.

In fairness, though, Australian news was pretty similar. Just more white faces and more sports. She realised she was staring at her mother, and looked away as the elder woman's eyes flicked up to her.

"Everything ok?" her mum asked. She was mending one of the twins' shirts, and Ila realised it had been one of hers once.

"Yep, all good." She went back to her books but felt her mother's eyes lingering on her. Ila sighed, there was no more putting it off. She just had to ask— no, tell her mum, what she was going to do.

"Mum?"

"Hmm?"

"Can I tell you something?" Her mum put down her work. "I was wondering if I could… well… I've been training heaps, you know, in the last few years and…"

Now the heavy eyes of her father fixed on her. Ila stood, hands clenched behind her back and doing her best not to wither under their questioning glare.

"Michael thinks I'm ready to step up to—"

"To what?" her mother's eyes locked on like lasers.

"Competing. There's this huge tournament coming up and—"

"We've already spoken about this." The lasers were burning through her.

"Yes, but, he thinks I should fight. He says I'm good enough to actually take it somewhere serious—"

Her father launched to his feet. "Fighting?"

"Yeah, Dad, you know… martial arts, Jiu jitsu… well, all of it really."

Now her mother was on her feet, her mending dropped to the floor.

Ila swallowed; this was what she'd feared. "It's only a sport," she offered.

Her father glared stupefied. "Sport?"

"Dad, I—"

"We fought, so that you wouldn't have to! And now you want to fight for sport?"

Without another word he marched past her. She wanted to call out to him, to try and make him understand but her voice left her.

Now her mother approached. Ila dropped her eyes as Rita took a thick law book from the kitchen table. She brandished it at her daughter, like a bible-bashing preacher. "Ila, this is hard for you to understand. You are still young. But *this...*" she slapped the book into her other hand. "This will get you somewhere. Not rolling around in a cage for the entertainment of idiots."

Tossing the book back on the desk, she lifted Ila's chin, her voice dangerous. "I've tolerated this nonsense for too long. I allowed you to do it because it seemed to give you confidence.

But now it is stealing you from your opportunity and your responsibility. You should be studying or working—"

"But that's all I do, Mum!"

"Enough! You have a chance that we gave everything for you to take! Abdul has missed it." Her voice was breaking. Ila could see tears building in the corners of her mum's eyes.

"Everything I do is for you! This is the one thing I have for myself!" Ila snatched up the book from the table. It was her turn to brandish it now. "I could be more than just this!"

"No," her mother finally said. "Not while you are living in this house."

Mother and daughter glowered at each other, both wanting to say more, but it was clear this was a fight Ila couldn't win.

Her mother never gave any quarter.

Defeated, she walked from the room. Hurrying down the hallway, she opened the front door and stepped out into the night. With no destination in mind, she ambled along the street.

A throbbing anxiety gripped her. She would never get to truly follow her path. Her true passion would be forever repressed beneath her parents' desires for her.

Beneath a buzzing streetlight, she stopped, slowly becoming aware of the sounds of the evening. Hip Hop droned from one of the houses nearby. A couple of drunken voices were yelling incoherently to one another. A police car turned the corner, cruising toward her, slowing as it passed. A pale face peered out at her suspiciously but the car drove on. Then she was alone and the noise around her forgotten.

Pulling her phone from her pocket, she scrolled through her messages and found Michael's name.

Fingers hovering over the keys of the phone, she breathed in the night air. She had to make the decision for herself, and she had to make it now.

You're either all in or not at all. There's no halfway.

She typed him her simple message. 'I'm in.'

Her thumb hovered over the send button. Her mum would never forgive her, and her father might not speak to her again. Was that really what she wanted?

No, it wasn't, but she hit send anyway.

CHAPTER 13

The Ute clunked to a stop in front of a sizable, industrial building on the corner of a desolate street. Rose frowned; this didn't look like a gym. David had said it was a gym, hadn't he? It looked more like a warehouse.

"You sure this is the right fucking address?" her dad spat.

She checked the email on her phone again and nodded. This was the place.

He screwed up his face in disgust. "What a shithole," he declared.

Rose cringed as he shifted in his seat beside her. She was always on edge around him now. His smell and the way his eyes lingered on her. Mumbling a goodbye, she snatched up her bag and opened the door.

His hand whipped across the space and caught the handle, preventing it from opening any further.

"Do I get a kiss goodbye?"

She gave him a peck on the cheek, and he released the door as she slid quickly out. "Hey!" he called as she crossed the street. "Don't fuck this up. I don't want any more pigs coming over to the house. Understand?"

After nodding to her father, the Ute rumbled away, and Rose took in the building. It was square and plain, with faded white paint covering red bricks. The windows were placed high, up near the roof so she couldn't sneak a look inside. Although there was one low window around the side of the building facing the adjoining street.

The glass on the front doors, looked like it hadn't ever been cleaned! The whole place had the feeling of an abandoned factory from some horror movie.

A rusted, faded sign hung over the door, creaking in the breeze. 'Duncan's Boxing and Martial Arts'.

Well, that was the name that was on the email. She rubbed at her neck. This didn't feel right. The place had the aura of a drug den rather than a business dedicated to health and fitness.

Still, David had given her the run-down, assured her it was legit, and warned her that the owner would be, "challenging".

"Despite all that, Rose," he'd said, "I have to be completely upfront with you. This really is your last option. There's nothing more I can do for you if this fails."

She made the slow walk up to the building then stepped through the grimy glass doors and into the gym. "Maybe I should've taken the jail option," she mumbled to herself.

*

Rose peered nervously around the cavernous space. Directly ahead was a front counter, behind which was a door with a window and the word, 'Office' painted across it. The place was deathly silent, and surprisingly chilly.

The main area of the gym had a large boxing ring. The

ropes hung slack and were wrapped with gaffer tape. Around the whole edge of the gym were punching bags, most of which were also held together by gaffer tape.

Her dad had once told her there was nothing in the world that gaffer tape couldn't fix.

She was surprised that it wasn't holding the crumbling walls together as well!

Mirrors were on every wall, except near the change room doors. The whole place was horribly dusty. Motes danced on rays of sunlight spilling through the high windows.

A spacious matted area was marked out on the far side, with pads lined up against the wall. She assumed these were for punching and kicking. This would've been a prime gym back in its day, but the faded posters on the walls of fighters she'd never heard of, and the rusted chains that held the crumbling punching bags to the ceiling, not to mention the sizable cracks in the concrete floor, told the story of a building housing relics from better days.

She moved to the counter. A poster caught her attention. It was fresh and new, like it had only just been put up.

"Warrior Heart Fighting Challenge," she read. "Ten thousand dollars prize money."

She attempted to peer into the back office, but it was pitch dark. "Hello?" she called timidly.

Nothing.

She hit the rusted bell on the counter.

Still nothing.

Was this all a big stitch up? She slapped the bell a few more times.

Yet still no response.

She raised her had to strike the bell again when the office door flew open.

A woman in a white tank top and black shorts appeared. "Hit that bell again, and I'll break your fingers off." It was more a statement of fact than a threat.

Rose lowered her hand. The woman who approached the desk smelled just like her dad after a night on the booze. Her dark hair spilled from beneath a red bandana, and her arms looked like they'd been chiselled out of rock. But the lines on her face betrayed her age, and her nose was slightly crooked. The result of taking some heavy punches at some stage in the past, Rose guessed.

Reaching under the counter, she tossed some papers in front of Rose. "You're David's brat, right?"

Rose nodded quickly.

"Sign these and then we'll get you started. How old are you?"

"Eighteen."

"And still in school?" The woman seemed to find that amusing. Rose swallowed the insult and signed the papers. "I'm Cathy. I'll be running your placement... or whatever the hell you want to call it. Follow!"

She led Rose toward the change rooms, pushing the door open. The smell that hit her made Rose gag.

"This is your office," Cathy stated, kicking a bucket toward her and tossing her a dirty mop.

Rose noticed a sly grin flash across Cathy's face. She was

enjoying this.

"You start at seven, you leave at five. All this will need to be spotless, and I will check it so don't cut any fucking corners. You're also responsible for cleaning the mats, the equipment, and front area. Stay out of the way and don't be late."

She stared flatly at Rose, who stared timidly back.

"Questions?" she asked.

Rose shook her head quickly, her eyes falling on Cathy's calloused knuckles. They looked rougher than bricks.

Cathy stalked out.

Jail was really starting to look like the better option.

CHAPTER 14

The day crawled along. Rose dusted, swept, and polished. But no matter how much she cleaned, the dust just kept drifting down to settle again and she'd have to start all over.

A few people began turning up to train, and she did her best to stay out of the way. Rose had always felt she could handle herself in most situations. Despite the fights she'd had at school, she knew most kids tried to stay clear of her, which was exactly how she liked it. Even when she was out on the street, she had confidence she could back herself if anything went down.

But seeing the steady stream of fighters enter during the afternoon, their bodies coated in tattoos and chiselled with wiry muscle, her confidence made a quick escape out the back door.

Cathy was training one woman in the ring, who seemed rather advanced in years. Yet the way the woman's limbs cracked the punching pads, and the lightning speed with which she threw her combinations was terrifying.

She's over twice my age, and she'd destroy me without breaking a sweat.

Rose moved to the mirrored wall. This way she could clean and still watch the fighters training in the ring.

The next person Cathy trained was a short guy, built like a fridge. Rose gawked, as Cathy ran him through a combination of strikes. He made it look so fluid.

Cathy had two large pads on her forearms with which she caught the kicks and punches, and Rose was amazed the woman remained standing through it. The guy's kicks landed with so much force, Rose felt it reverberate through her body, even though she was at least ten meters away.

She watched as Cathy called out a combination. "Ok, jab, straight right, roundhouse and right elbow, go!"

The guy nodded and unleashed the blistering assault.

Rose observed closely. Then she positioned herself in front of one of the bags. She threw the combination slowly, and very awkwardly, but she was surprised at how crisply her kick landed. She smiled; hitting the bag felt good.

"Hey!"

Rose jumped halfway to the ceiling. Cathy glared down at Rose from the ring, face flushed red. Sweat dripped from her forehead, her bandana dark with perspiration.

"Did you empty the bins?"

Rose snatched up her rag and spray bottle, almost sprinting away. This was a brutal new world for her, and Cathy was the queen.

*

Slipping into the office, a bin bag clasped in her hand, Rose made her way to the desk, which sat in the centre of the room and was covered in papers and bills. A couch was squashed under the window, and there was a bar fridge and rusty kettle near the sink.

She had a sneaking suspicion that this might also double as Cathy's bedroom. But maybe the woman just spent a lot of time here.

Emptying the over-flowing waste bin into the bin bag, she spotted a picture framed on the desk. A girl, dressed in what she guessed was a Karate uniform, held a trophy that was almost the same size as her. A stout looking man stood with his arm around her, a proud smile etched across his face. The girl must have been a young Cathy, and the man her father?

Her attention fell on a locker against the wall. The door was slightly a jar with dark pieces of cloth hanging within.

Frowning, she checked the door to make sure Cathy was still busy out in the gym then poked her head in for a closer look. A faded Karate uniform hung on a coat hanger, and a pair of black silk shorts with some kind of Asian writing across them, hung nearby. Next to these hung four different strips of black cloth. She looked back at the photo and clicked.

These were Karate belts!

All black, that meant expert level, right? And Cathy had four of them. Did that mean she knew four different types of martial arts? Shutting the locker door, she all but ran from the office. Last thing she needed was to be caught snooping by a four-time black belt!

*

Mercifully, the day came to an end. The gym would be open late, but Rose had done her first ten-hours of torture for the day.

Only one hundred and ninety hours left, she thought with a sigh.

Heading toward the counter, she stopped before one of the punching bags and glanced around. Cathy was busy talking with one of the gym goers.

Rose stood in front of the bag. Stepping her left foot out, she pivoted and kicked the bag with a round house. She was pleased when it connected with a solid thump!

"Nice kick."

Wheeling around to the gruff voice, she was confronted by Cathy, leaning on the wall, slightly obscured by the other punching bags.

"Done some training?" Cathy asked.

"Um… I did Taekwondo… when I was a kid," she replied nervously.

Cathy nodded, walked over to the bag and held it in place. "Do it again."

Rose hesitated, but Cathy nodded for her to go ahead.

Setting herself, she threw the kick as hard as she could. *Thump!* Rose felt a jolt of pride as she landed the strike solidly.

Cathy's hand flew out, slapping her hard across the cheek.

Rose stared at her in complete shock.

"Keep your hands up," Cathy muttered and walked off without looking back.

"You… you can't do that!" Rose stammered. It was more

the shock, then the pain that hurt her. The psycho couldn't do that to her! Could she?

Cathy walked into her office. "You won't drop your hands again though, will you?"

Rose shook her head in disbelief, grabbing her bag and hurrying to the exit. She'd had more than enough of this for one day, but then the door to the gym swung open and a man dressed in a perfectly tailored suit sauntered in, fixing her with a wide smile as he approached.

"Hey kiddo, is Cathy in?" he asked genially. He was short; his hair slicked back, his face round and confidant. His whole look screamed dodgy car salesman.

Cathy reappeared from the office and her face dropped. "You can go," she said to Rose.

She moved a few paces away but listened as the pair spoke. The man spread his hands wide. "Ah, there she is! The old Brown Bomber herself!"

"What do you want, Ange?" she folded her arms. Cathy's energy was dangerous even at rest, but this man acted like they were old friends.

"Well, it would be nice to get a text or an email back," he said.

"Been busy," she muttered darkly.

He raised an eyebrow at the almost deserted training area. "Clearly!" His smile took on a slightly more sinister edge as he laid his hands on the counter. "You know, I can still remember that last tournament you fought in. That was some real-life Karate Kid shit! Man, you were throwing them so fast those other girls were dropping before they knew what hit them."

Cathy shifted uncomfortably. It was obvious to Rose that this man was touching on something that she wasn't keen on revisiting.

"Your dad was beaming! Old Duncan White knew his girl was going to be a champion."

Cathy offered a half-hearted smile.

"I'm sorry," Ange said. "I get very... what's the word? *Nostalgic,* when I come here. Anyway, enough of that! You given any thought to my proposal?"

Cathy looked away. "I need more time."

"It's been a few months."

"I can't just pack this all up—"

"I'm simply trying to offer a solution out of this fix you're in." He lent forward and Rose had to strain to hear him. "This whole area is getting developed. And this spot is prime real estate. You give it over to me. I sell it to my connections and turn a profit. You can go and set up somewhere else. It's only bricks and mortar after all."

She nodded sadly. But then her eyes shot up, that dangerous gaze in them again. "Yeah, well, I get very *nostalgic* too."

His smile faded to a sneer. "I need that eleven thousand you owe, plus the interest. I've been more than patient because of your father and the respect I owe him, God rest his soul. But this whole situation is wearing pretty bloody thin." He tapped the desk, and straightened his suit. "I'll be seeing you again real soon Bomber."

He left and Rose took the opportunity to leave too.

As she hurried around the side of the gym, she passed the one window that looked out from the office. Cathy was at her desk, drinking from a large Vodka bottle. Keeping her head down, Rose hurried on. There were things going on here that she knew she needed to stay clear of. *Just one hundred and ninety more hours,* she reminded herself.

There was still a long way to go.

CHAPTER 15

Ila had headed out for dinner with some of the other students from Michael's Dojo, and had loved every second of it. After what had happened with her parents, she was just happy to be out of her study-work bubble. She was just a regular young woman, doing regular things other young people did.

The reaction of her parents still played in her thoughts, but she pushed it aside.

With the meal now over, they stood out the front of the local eatery saying their farewells to the others, and she soon found herself walking with Michael.

For a while neither said anything.

He broke the silence first as they headed down the quiet city street. "I... am... stuffed!" he said, rubbing his stomach.

"You need to remember to breathe between bites," she said with a laugh.

His smile dropped, and he stopped her with a touch. "So, your folks are ok with this?"

Her look said it all. His frustration was palpable. "Is this going to be a problem?"

"So long as my Uni grades don't drop, it'll be fine."

"Remember what I said about being all in?"

"I can handle it," she said. "Trust me."

His eyes said he wasn't happy. "Well," he continued, "the good news is that I've managed to get you some sparring time at a gym just over on the North side. It's really old school, pretty rough woman who runs the place too. But it will get you used to people trying to rip your head off."

"Did you recruit my mum?" she said with a grin.

But Michael was all business. "Listen, Ila, I don't want you to feel pressured into this. If you really don't want to do it, I'll understand—"

"No," she said firmly. "I've made my choice. I'm doing this for me. I actually feel really positive about—"

Something solid barged into her back causing her to gasp in shock and pain. Stumbling forward, Michael caught her and helped her to straighten up. Spinning around she saw two, middle-aged men walking past. Their faces were locked on to hers, dark eyes hateful and challenging.

"Aw, sorry," slurred the eldest of the two. "Didn't see you there. You lot just seem to disappear at night."

They slowed their pace. It was clear they were looking for a challenge, a reason to fight. Her body pumped with adrenaline, as she took them in. They were both around forty, and both looked and smelled as if they'd been doing some heavy drinking.

Michael was suddenly in front of her. "You just bumped her deliberately asshole!"

"Aw, did I?" the man and his friend faced up to them. "You

going to do something?" he growled.

Michael's eyes narrowed. He stalked forward, but she caught his hand. "Leave it," she whispered.

The elder of the two laughed cruelly. "You should listen to your black princess, mate."

Michael's body tensed. While Michael would easily take these two apart, Ila also knew how the law operated – she was studying it after all. If he hurt them, he'd lose everything. His gym, his training license, and everything that he'd worked hard for over the last ten years.

All these guys would have to do was state that they'd accidentally bumped into her, and that Michael had gone nuts. Or worse, they might even get a lucky shot in and Michael could get hurt. Either way, it was a no-win situation and she knew it.

All this flashed through her thoughts in a breath. She gripped his hand tighter. "Please, just leave it."

His eyes drifted to hers. She could read his anger in them. He stepped back with a frustrated grunt.

The two men laughed. "Didn't think so." The elder one wasn't done though. "You people need to stay out of our fucking way," he said, jabbing a finger at her.

Ila held his gaze, and breathed, holding her chin high.

"Come on man, fuck these two, let's go," his friend said.

"Nah, not yet," the older one said. He squared up on her. "I want an apology from *you*, for bumping into *me.*"

Michael lurched forward again, and this time Ila had to put herself between him and the aggressor. "You gotta be fucking kidding me!" Michael seethed, his hands clenched tightly. She gripped his wrist, and he went silent but she could hear the rasping of his breath, see the way his body coiled like an iron spring.

Ila steadied herself, and smiled politely at the man. Supressing her own anger and fear, she took these too in. She could handle this without throwing punches. "I'm so sorry," she said pleasantly. "I hope you didn't hurt yourself."

He chuckled triumphantly at his friend. But she wasn't done.

"A gentleman of your age, the last thing I'd want to do is… hurt you," she whispered darkly. The pleasant smile was still stretched across her lips. However, the veiled threat behind her words was not lost on him.

He looked her up and down, his eyes suddenly darting from her to Michael. His friend pulled on his arm, "Come on, mate. Just let it go!"

"You just remember whose country you're in!" he blurted out. They moved off fast before either her or Michael could respond.

Michael moved to follow them.

"Leave it. It's nothing."

"Nothing? Ila they just—"

"Michael. Please…"

"But—"

"They're just drunk. Don't worry about it. I need to get going. I'll see you soon."

She took both his hands and kissed him on the cheek.

"Ila?"

"I'm fine, really. I just have to get home." She gave him a flash of a warm smile and hurried off. She saw him move to pursue the men, but then his shoulders slumped, and he turned away.

Ila quickened her pace; she didn't want him to see her cry.

*

Arriving home, she stole down the hall toward her room. Despite her efforts to convince herself that the incident on the street hadn't really affected her, a horrible numbness had settled in her mind. How could they hate her so much? Those men didn't even know her.

Abdul suddenly emerged from the kitchen, glazed eyes fixing on her. Obviously, he'd been smoking weed in the backyard.

"Look who's been out late," he said with a wink. "You get some private sessions with the coach?"

She ignored him, desperate to get to her room before the tears that had been threating to fall the whole way home, fell.

"Oi? What's up your ass?" he pressed angrily. Closing the door on him, she fell on to her bed, her heart thumping, her thoughts racing, and her anger burning bright.

It wasn't the first time she'd dealt with racism. And it wasn't even what they had said. It was the sheer hatred they had for her. She had seen it lit like fire in their eyes, felt it vibrating from their whole being.

All directed at her.

In return, she had almost been ready to... well... she didn't want to admit to herself what she might have done to them.

Ila opened one of the law books by her bed but couldn't bring herself to read it.

Her door clicked opened gently. Abdul was there. She felt him eyeing her, weighing up what must've happened.

"I know that look," he whispered, as he sat next to her.

After a moment, he took the book and laid it to the side. Putting his arm around her, she rested her head on his shoulder, and allowed her tears to finally fall.

CHAPTER 16

R ose had fallen into a solid routine at the gym. Arriving at seven on the dot, she'd organise all her cleaning equipment, and then get to work. Cathy allowed her a short break in the morning and a longer one around midday.

Now she was hanging out towels she'd run through the wash. Cathy had just finished training a client, her bandana once again dark with sweat. Slipping out of the ring, the woman snatched one of the freshly cleaned towels from the drying rack, wiped her face and under her arms. She then tossed it back to Rose, who stared at it in disgust.

Really?

Rose took the grizzled coach in. Cathy still had a fighter's physique, and a few scars lined her cheeks but her eyes had that glazed redness she often saw in her dad's. Rose knew a seasoned drinker when she saw one.

"Did you used to fight?" Rose found herself asking.

Cathy gave her a sideways glance. "Yeah."

"We're you… you know, good?"

The grizzled trainer rounded on her. "Want to jump in the ring and find out?"

Rose gripped the towel she was holding protectively. Why'd she start asking this psycho questions? Wasn't the plan to just keep her head down and get through this shit?

Cathy erupted with a deep belly laugh. "Relax, I'm just messing with you kid!" She snatched up another towel and wiped under her arms again. She then tossed it back to Rose who visibly recoiled.

"You're pretty forward, aren't you?" Cathy continued. "Is that why you keep getting into scraps?"

Rose shrugged.

"You think you're hard or something?" Cathy pressed.

Rose frowned. "No."

"So why do you bash people?"

"I don't bash people!"

"What are you doing here then?"

"Because I fucking have to be here!"

"Yeah, because you like to bash people."

Rose's anger swelled again. This old bitch couldn't talk to her like that. Black belt or not, she was ready to swing on this fossil and to hell with the consequences. She'd rather do the jail time. "What the fuck would you know?" Rose challenged. She turned and walked to grab her bag and get the hell out of this shithole.

"Ok, I'll tell David you quit," Cathy said with a shrug.

Rose quickly sobered to the reality of her situation. David would report it to the courts. She'd be done. For all her talk of wanting to do the jail time instead, the reality was she was eighteen. There would be no juvenile detention this time.

Cathy shook her head with a click of her tongue. "You need to cool that fire, kid. Can't go around punching everything that makes your life difficult."

Rose gave a terse nod, but she was still supressing the growing rage.

"Go and have a break," Cathy said, turning on her heel and walking away.

But Rose returned to sorting the towels in a small act of defiance. She heard Cathy give a sniff of approval.

*

Ensuring the old coach was focused on the fighter she was training, Rose abandoned her cleaning duties, and moved to the punching bag to practice. Left hook, right kick. She noticed the fighter pushed his hip forward when he kicked. She tried this, and the bag went flying back.

She tried again, with her weaker left leg. Rose launched the kick, and opened up her hip as she did. The bag almost buckled from the power. Rose hopped up and down with excitement at the discovery.

"You gonna use that in the school yard?"

Cathy and the fighter were leaning on the ropes of the ring watching her.

Rose said nothing.

Cathy gave one of her knowing half smiles. "Listen, when you do that round-house, step your foot to forty-five degrees out. Not just straight out to the side like you're doing. Then pivot on the ball of your foot. Swing the kick like you're bringing it all the way through the bag. Don't just kick the bag, kick *through* the bag."

Surprised she wasn't copping an ear bashing, Rose gave the advice a shot.

Crack!

The bag rippled with the impact of her kick. The fighter let out an impressed whistle. Cathy slid out of the ring, dropped her pads and took hold of the bag.

"Again!" Cathy yelled. "Open up even more!"

Rose unleashed the kick, as she did, Cathy threw a hand out to slap her. But this time Rose blocked the slap. The older woman smiled slyly. "Nice work, we'll have to try it on the pads soon."

She headed back to the ring. Rose threw a few more kicks until Cathy's voice broke the air. "Oi! You emptied the bins?"

CHAPTER 17

Tonight was an advanced class, meaning there were no white or blue belts, only purple, brown and black belts at the dojo.

Ila lived for this class. It was her chance to try herself against the best students.

Sixty minutes of non-stop sparring broken into five-minute rounds. It was exhausting, but also exhilarating.

As she rolled with her training partners, many of whom she'd known for years, a raging heat burned within her. She kept seeing the faces of the two men who'd abused her on the street, and her initial melancholy was now replaced with anger. A little voice of reason inside implored her to calm down. She and Michael had been in the wrong place at the wrong time. That was all. And why was she taking it out on her training partners anyway?

Besides, no one had gotten hurt. Well, not physically at least. So why was she so worked up? Was it because it now seemed that Abdul had been right? No, it was a one-off thing... just like every other time this shit happened.

She wiped sweat from her eyes.

Across the mats one of the brown belts was waving her over to roll.

This was just what she needed. A challenge.

The woman smiled up at her as she approached. Jessica had helped her out when she'd started training. Her smile hid a fierce but fair and driven person.

Ila didn't return the smile.

She wanted to win this round and beat the higher rank. Then she'd feel strong again.

Jessica flashed her an uncertain look as they slapped hands, but she focused and the two began to circle. Ila felt Michael's gaze on them, and she intended to show him just what she was capable of.

The pair locked up, and Ila dove in for an immediate submission. But Jessica saw it coming and countered. Before Ila knew what exactly had happened, Jessica had her pinned and was in full control.

Ila scrapped rather than trying to use technique to escape. She could hear Michael barking instructions from the side of the mats.

But his words bounced away.

Just submit her, she's not that good. Come on, fight! Fight, goddamn it!

Eventually she managed a messy escape but Jessica still had her trapped in her guard position. Again, Ila went for an almost impossible submission, attempting a choke without even being able to lock her hands together.

"No, Ila! Come on," Michael called, rubbing his eyes

angrily. "Break her guard first, gain a stronger position, and then try for the submission! You know all this!"

But she scrapped on, trying to out muscle her more seasoned opponent.

Jessica stayed calm and calculating. Ila sensed the woman had gone into a real competitive mode, and that meant she was in trouble.

Inch by inch, Jessica worked herself into the dominant position again.

To Ila's frustration the shorter woman now swept her. Pulling Ila forward and leaping onto her back. Jessica hooked her legs around Ila's waist, and her arm under Ila's neck.

Jessica rolled on to her side and applied the rear naked choke. Slowly squeezing, adding more and more pressure. Ila's airway was being squashed, but she refused to tap out. She battled to drag Jessica's arm away from her neck. But the more experienced fighter was in complete control.

Michael called from the sidelines again. "Tap out, Ila. She's got you!"

Ila strained, desperate to wrestle the offending arm off her windpipe, but now white splotches were appearing in her vision, and the room was slowly going dark.

"She won't tap!" Jessica called to Michael.

Michael gave a shake of the head and then nodded to Jessica. The brown belt squeezed harder.

Ila's eyes rolled back in her head. The white splotches were replaced by complete darkness.

*

Her head spun as she came out of the darkness. She lay flat on her back, Jessica gazing down at her like a disapproving mother. "Why the hell didn't you just tap out?" the brown belt demanded.

Ila dragged herself up to sitting. With her braids hanging over her face, and her Gi dishevelled, she must look exactly how she felt, a complete mess.

"Sorry," she mumbled, and grabbed her purple belt from the floor, where it had come away during the round.

Michael wouldn't even look at her as she shuffled off to the change rooms beaten and humiliated.

*

It didn't matter that she'd lost. What mattered was that she'd had the mindset to try and hurt her training partners, her friends. She wanted to apologise, but just couldn't pluck up the courage to face them. So she hid in the bathroom wallowing in her guilt. After she'd heard most of the others leave, Ila wandered out into the gym area.

Michael was waiting, arms folded across his chest. His eyes shining bright with repressed anger. "What the hell was that about?" he demanded.

She cast her eyes to the ground. "I'm sorry."

"You can't let emotions trap you," he snapped.

"Like you did the other night?"

He ignored her and continued. "These classes are a chance for you to develop those ground skills we've worked on against serious competition," he said. "And tonight, you just threw it all away. You ignored all the strategies we've spent months slaving over! Tonight, you just wanted to scrap. You were as bad as that guy you humiliated on the mat the other day."

He gave a dismissive shake of his head and moved away. "Your first amateur fight isn't far off. So try and get your head on properly, will you?"

Slamming the door of his office behind him, he effectively shut out any rebuke she might have attempted.

Stepping into the humid night, she headed home to the other family she was disappointing.

CHAPTER 18

Rose knew she was pushing her luck with her dad by going out again with Petra. However, unlike the party from the other week that had ended in a punch up, this one had been a complete fizzer.

A few kids from her school had turned up, but most hadn't bothered and instead had headed to the city. Neither she, nor Petra was particularly keen on having to get in and out of town that night. So, they'd stolen a few drinks each instead and sat on the play equipment at the park. They chatted, drank, and gazed at the lights from the cars crossing the City Link bridge in the distance.

Soon they were walking the short distance back home. Rose realised how slow their pace was. It was like neither of them wanted to get home too quickly, and Rose was certainly happy to prolong her time with her Turkish beauty.

That strange, but pleasant nervousness swept through her as she watched Petra scroll through her phone, the glow from the screen shining off her dark eyes.

As they talked, Petra would flash her a cheeky grin every now and then, and Rose found herself feeling like she was swimming in those mischievous dark eyes.

Realising that Petra was mid-sentence, she forced herself to listen, and cease her musings.

"...fuck, babe, if he finds out it was me who sent that message, I'll die! Like literally die! RIP me!"

Rose laughed along with her. The sound echoed around the empty suburban streets, then she felt Petra's energy switch, and her friend actually put her phone away.

"You know, Tierney still hasn't come back yet?"

"So?" Rose sniffed.

"Just thought you should know."

"Fuck her."

"Jesus, settled down Elsa, fucking ice queen over here," Petra said. "Anyway, how's your placement thing going?" she asked, switching her questioning.

Rose shrugged. "Its ok, the owner is pretty scary, but kind of cool. She might even let me do some training."

Petra erupted in laughter. "Ha! Fuck off! Has she met you? Seriously, you're like Connor McGregor's sister minus the mouth. She must be nuts training you up."

They arrived near the front of Rose's house, making sure to drop their voices – they didn't want to wake her dad. Although he was probably black-out drunk, considering Collingwood had been victorious again earlier in the night.

Rose reached out and hugged Petra. To her excitement, the shorter girl returned the hug. She gripped Petra tightly, feeling a rush of warmth through her body. She knew it was getting weirder for Petra the longer she held the embrace. But she just didn't want to let go.

"Fuck, Rosie, you're crushing me," Petra's muffled voice said from down near Rose's chest.

"I've been missing you P," she said releasing her.

Petra, was seemingly oblivious to Rose's attempted intimacy. She'd already retrieved her phone again. "I understand," said Petra smugly. "Life gets pretty boring without me, and you are just a basic bitch after all. You can't help it."

Rose stole another quick hug before Petra was off down the street, head buried back in her phone. "I'll text you tomorrow," Rose called softly.

She took a deep breath. These feelings or ideas, or... *whatever* the hell it was she was having, she just had to be careful. She didn't want to make things awkward between them.

Rose scratched in frustration at her forehead. What was she doing? What did she want out from her friend? Was 'friend' even the right word to use?

Get a grip! She chastised herself as she snuck inside.

*

Over her many years of sneaking out to parties, Rose had mastered the art of entering the house quietly. With the slickness and silence of a master burglar, she unlocked the screen and front door, slipped inside and closed them without a sound.

Sliding off her shoes, she crept across the living room carpet toward the hallway. A noise came to her, blanketed and strained, like someone was attempting to muffle it.

Frowning into the darkness, Rose could see something moving up against the fridge in the kitchen.

Confused, she padded forward and peered into the black of the kitchen. The noise was becoming clearer now.

A solid, rhythmic bumping sound broke the silence of the night. But it was when she heard a very familiar, pained moan that a horror came over her.

Jo!

Slapping on the light switch, she squinted against the harsh neon flare as the brutal tableau was illuminated before her.

Her dad had Jo pinned against the fridge, in a painfully contorted position, with his pants around his ankles and his hand covering her mouth.

Both his and Jo's voices overlapped when they spotted her in the doorway.

"Rosie! Go to your room, please love!" Jo's muffled scream came.

"Where the fuck did you come from!" Her dad cried, struggling to pull his pants up.

Jo pulled her dressing gown around her, eyes red with tears. "Rosie! Just go to your room," she pleaded. But rage erupted within her. She faced her father, saw his mouth moving, and his hands gesturing at her wildly.

She focused the eruption squarely on him. Everything became a red mist of hate, as she rushed him. All she wanted was to inflict pain. To hurt him the way he hurt everyone else.

Crashing into him, she threw what she thought would be devastating punches. Although caught unprepared, her strikes bounced away as if she were hitting a wall.

His hands snatched at her. She was hoisted into the air and

then, *BANG!* She was driven into the cold linoleum floor. Pain shot through her back as her breath escaped.

He was atop her. One hand was around her throat, the other turning her face away and pressing it into the floor. The pressure on the side of her head was horrific. It truly felt like the bones in her skull would crack open!

"Don't raise your hands to me, girl! Do you understand?" he hissed into her ear.

She shrieked in pain, but he continued to press his weight on her.

Jo was by their side now. "Dan! She's your fucking daughter! Please!"

He ignored her and leant in closer. There was the familiar sickly smell of bourbon and coke on his breath. "I want to hear you say it," he said. His voice was terrifyingly calm and composed. Jo was screaming at him and trying to pull his hand from around her throat. But he pushed down harder on the unyielding surface.

The fight went out of her. The fire of rage doused. "Yes!" she screamed.

"Yes, what?" he growled. A drop of spittle hit her face.

"Yes! I understand!"

He released her, stood and pressed his bare foot on her chest. "See where you are now, Rosie? That's where you belong."

A light step caught their attention. They all fell to silence. Beth appeared wide-eyed in the doorway. The child was quivering, her tiny hands gripping the doorframe.

Their father stepped off her, and walked out of the room as if nothing had happened.

Jo pulled Rosie to her in a tight embrace.

Beth dashed toward them, throwing herself into Rose's arms.

She held her sister tenderly, the little girl's tears staining Rose's shirt.

The three of them huddled on the unforgiving linoleum floor until they heard snoring drifting from the bedroom, and they quietly made their way into Rose's room.

Curling up in the single bed, they waited for the dawn.

CHAPTER 19

C athy greeted her with a scowl at the front counter when she entered. Rose mumbled her apology and moved to grab her cleaning gear. But Cathy stepped in front of her. "Cutting it fine, aren't you?"

She hid her bruised face behind her hair. Rose really didn't want to deal with the questions that the bruise would certainly raise. Last thing she needed was the cops back at their place. Her dad would lose it something savage.

Cathy tilted her head to look into her face.

Rose shied away, but it was too late. The coach brushed her hair back, and cringed at the sight of the red and purple contusion covering the side of her face.

"You been fighting?" she asked, her voice bubbling with anger. "Because if you have, you can just fuck off right now! I don't need to deal with that shit. I was doing David a favour bringing you in here—"

"No!"

"What?"

"No, I haven't been fighting."

Cathy's knowing eyes scanned her up and down. She could

almost see the gears clicking in the coach's head as she put all the evidence together. Letting out a long breath, her grim face softened. Rose could tell from the way Cathy's posture slumped, that she knew what had happened, and that she'd seen it many times before.

"Let me guess," Cathy said softly. "You walked into a door at home?"

Rose wanted to tell the truth but again, the fear came. The fear of the cops becoming involved, and the way her dad would respond after they'd left. It all played out before her like a horror movie.

Rose shook her head. "Don't worry," she said trying to move away. "It's nothing."

"You want to tell me who did that to you?"

Rose shook her head quickly again.

Cathy chewed her lip in concern, and Rose knew she had to think of something or the coach would be on the phone to David or the cops in a heartbeat.

"It's not what you think. I just got jumped by a kid from my school," she lied.

Cathy nodded slowly. But her eyes gave away her thoughts. She knew Rose was lying.

A sudden thought hit Rose as her eyes fell on the ring in the centre of the gym. Before she could stop herself she was speaking earnestly. "Would you teach me how to fight?"

"Why? So you can use it on whoever did that to you?"

Rose waved her away. "Forget it then," she said, heading to the change rooms.

"I could," Cathy said simply, fingers tapping her chin in thought. "But if I train you, and that is a big *if*, there's some stuff you need to do first to show me you're serious."

As she spoke, she moved over to the front desk, opening the first aid box on the counter. Rose returned, and was all ears.

"This arvo, go to the park down the road and run five kilometres. Then you come back here and finish your work. You do that for the rest of the week, then maybe... *maybe* I'll train you."

Cathy cracked an instant ice pack, slapping it into Rose's hand. She then pressed the hand to the bulging bruise. "Fighting isn't about being the toughest or meanest, it's about dedication. If you can show me that you're dedicated to it, then I will dedicate the time to you." Her gaze held Rose's. "You sure you don't want to tell me who did that?" she asked in a gentler tone.

Rose shook her head. "Like I said, it was just some kid from school."

"Well, you tell me if this kid does it again."

"It's only a scratch."

"Yeah, well, it's the scratches on the inside that I'm worried about." Cathy sighed and gripped Rose's shoulder. "You're a tough one, kid, but being tough isn't about pretending this shit isn't happening. The toughest people are the ones who have the courage to ask for help."

With a nod, Cathy headed into her office leaving Rose to dwell on her words.

CHAPTER 20

Never in her life had Rose done something as brutal, as utterly soul destroying, as this simple run around the park. She was huffing just one kilometre into the run, which for her was more of a staggered trot. People were literally walking faster than she was running!

One woman, easily over fifty, jogged passed with barely even a drop of sweat on her brow.

Rose stopped at a drink fountain, slurping down the water like it was the last drop on earth. Why the hell was Cathy forcing her to do this? What was the point? Then she remembered Cathy's little speech on discipline. This was a test, right?

The grizzled old bitch was trying to break her early, so she wouldn't have to train her. The realisation gave her the spark she needed. She wasn't giving up and going back to cleaning the stupid toilets.

No. Cathy was going to train her.

Then she'd be able to protect Beth and Jo. The thought of them alone at home, walking on eggshells around that prick ignited the spark to a flame.

Rose sucked down another gulp of water, and set off again

around the park. *You have to prove yourself to her.*

When she was done, her legs were burning, and no matter how many deep breaths she took, her lungs kept screaming for air. Slumping down next to the water fountain, she attempted to slow her pounding heart.

"This... is... fu... fucked," she muttered between breaths.

"Don't worry," a voice called. She looked up to see the pleasant, smiling face of the woman who had jogged passed her earlier. "You get better the more you do it."

The woman gave her a wink and jogged on.

"No shit?" Rose mumbled.

She limped back to the gym, cursing whichever sadistic prick it was that invented running.

CHAPTER 21

I t sounded like a pub brawl had broken out in the gym! Rose hurried through the front doors to see what was happening. A man stood up on the ring in one corner, and Cathy was on the opposite corner. Both were barking orders at two male fighters in the ring, who were sparring in full gear. Surrounding the ring were other fighters watching or warming up. Never before had she seen this amount of people in the gym at one time.

She decided it was best to keep a respectful distance.

Despite both fighters wearing shin protectors, boxing gloves and head guards, the blows they punished each other with echoed through the gym like gunshots.

Finally, the bell sounded and both men dropped to their knees, puffing desperately.

"Right!" Cathy bellowed, clapping her hands together. "Let's mix it up and get the ladies in!"

The other trainer nodded his approval and beckoned an African girl over, who stepped up to the ring confidently, moving with a fluid and strong gait.

"Hey, Cathy," the other trainer called. "Let's use the MMA

gloves, and add in the take downs."

Cathy nodded. "All right, but Lucy here knows her ground game," she said, gesturing to her own fighter, a lithe-looking woman who Rose hadn't seen at the gym before.

Cathy whispered some instructions to Lucy before slapping on a head guard.

What the hell was 'ground game'? Rose wondered as she moved to the side of the ring for a clear view.

The bell sounded. The two girls touched gloves and stepped back. Cathy's fighter, Lucy, came at the African girl like a tornado. She threw down combinations of kicks and punches, which connected sharply.

The African girl fielded a few hard shots, and Rose winced as one kick from Lucy smacked into the girl's temple. So powerful was the shot, it almost spun her head guard around.

Then Lucy did something Rose hadn't seen before. Dropping to one knee she tackled the girl's legs out from under her. Rose gawked as the pair wrestled on the ground. Was this allowed? They both seemed to be trying to twist each other's arms. What exactly were the rules here? Lucy definitely had the upper hand; at least that was how it seemed. How much longer could the other girl hold on with Lucy trying to rip her arm out of its socket?

"Ila!" the other trainer called out. "Recover guard!"

The African girl managed to wrap her legs around Lucy, pulling her down on top of her.

Rose raised a questioning eyebrow. What the hell was she doing? That seemed a bit... intimate for a fight.

"Kimora!" the other trainer yelled. "You've got her!"

Rose stared in awe as the African fighter, Ila, grabbed Lucy's wrist and twisted it behind her back.

Lucy immediately started slapping the ground, "Tap! Tap!" she called. The other girl released her, and the pair struggled up.

Cathy slapped the ropes in frustration. The other trainer clapped Ila on the back excitedly.

The fighters shook hands and started pulling off their gear. Rose just sat there staring. Never had she seen fighting like this! That a fighter could be pinned and yet somehow actually win the fight was something that she just couldn't wrap her head around.

"Hey!" Cathy called out. Rose jerked to attention. "Grab some ice!" she pointed to the African girl. The shot she'd taken to the head had split the skin around the temple.

Rose hurried to do so, still trying to understand what she'd just seen.

CHAPTER 22

Leaning into the stretch, Ila winced as her hamstring ached angrily in protest. A dark-haired girl approached holding ice wrapped in a towel.

"Do you need this?" she asked.

Ila smiled up at the kid and took the ice. "Thanks." She spotted the nasty looking bruise on the side of the girl's head as she turned away. "Are you sparring at all today?" she asked.

The girl looked back blankly. "Oh... nah, I'm not a fighter or anything."

"I just saw the bruise and thought... Never mind. Hey, thanks for the ice. I need it," she said, nodding her thanks again. The poor kid looked a bit intimidated by all the fighters milling around the ring.

She noticed the girl's hand go to the bruise on the side of her head. "Can I ask you something?" she said.

Ila nodded.

"What's all that wrestling stuff you two were doing near the end? Is that MMA?"

Ila stifled a laugh. "Not quite, it's Jiu Jitsu. Brazilian Jiu Jitsu."

"Is it hard to learn?"

Girl, you got no idea how hard! She gave another friendly grin. "It's difficult, but not impossible. You never really stop learning it, I guess." As she turned to the mirror to ice her cut, she saw just how bad her own bruising was around the temple. Her mum was going to kill her... if this sparring session didn't do it first.

"We look like twins!" the kid said. She was standing slightly behind Ila so she could be seen in the reflection.

Ila stared at the pale-skinned, dark-haired girl standing behind her, "Twins?"

The girl tapped her own bruise, which Ila realised was in the same spot as hers. She snickered. "Right, I thought you meant something else for a second there."

"Hey!" They both spun around to the ring, where Cathy was leaning on the ropes, tying up another fighter's gloves. "You emptied the bins or what? You're here to work, not socialise!"

The kid dashed off.

Ila returned to examining her bruise. She noticed a few more bumps and grazes starting to blossom on her face. Anxiety rippled through her, and she breathed deeply. No amount of makeup was going to hide these.

Ila wasn't sure what was worse, the beating she'd just taken in the ring, or the verbal beat down she'd endure when she returned home.

She pressed the ice down hard and lay back on the mats.

No one said it would be easy.

CHAPTER 22

The house was filled with its usual ruckus. Ila used the cover of the noise to slip in as quietly as possible.

"Ila?" her mum called from the kitchen.

She made a dash for the bathroom before her mum got a look at her face, and she would've made it to, but Abdul just happened to step out of his room as she passed.

"Holy shit!" he laughed. "That's one hell of a shiner! What does the other guy look like?"

Of all the nights he decides to stay home!

The clang of dishes being dumped in the sink, and her mother's furious steps meant she was trapped.

Rita stormed into the hall. "Ila? Come here."

"I just want to have a shower and change—"

"Here! Now!" Rita demanded, jabbing a finger at the ground in front of her.

Ila flashed Abdul a defeated glare. He swallowed hard at the realisation he'd just dropped her in the shit.

Trying to keep her hair covering the bruise, she walked to her mother. But her mum lifted her chin and pushed her hair out the way.

Her face contorted instantly into a mask of suppressed anger.

Ila tried desperately to think of something to say. "It's just from a stupid accident... um... at Uni. I fell and—"

"Don't lie to me!" Rita stamped her foot, the resounding thump echoing through the house.

Her father's head shot up and the twins were suddenly silent where they sat at the kitchen table.

Rita waved a quivering finger in her daughter's face. "I told you, no more! From now on you stick to your studies and your work and that's all!"

She snatched Ila's bag from her, and bustled through the kitchen to the back door of the house. "You *will* make something of your life!" she yelled.

"Mum, wait! What are you doing?" she hurried to follow. Abdul came too, but the twins scattered out of their mother's way. They knew when to make themselves scarce.

A heavy sinking feeling dropped into the pit of Ila's stomach. She hadn't seen her mum this furious since the first night the police brought Abdul home a few years back.

"Please! What are you doing?" she begged. But her mother ignored her, throwing open the door and stomping into their cramped back yard.

Ila felt the thousand eyes of the commission flats watching the scene. Her mother opened the lid of the waste bin, tipped the contents of Ila's bag on the ground and held up her Gi to her, then threw it into the bin.

"Mum! Calm down," Abdul said, pushing his way forward.

Ignoring her son, she took Ila's purple belt from where it had fallen on the ground. "Is this more important than your future?" she brandished it like a scrap of rubbish.

"It's part of my future!" Ila protested.

"You need to get your priorities right. And this is not one of them." Ila let out a cry as Rita threw the belt into the bin and slammed the lid shut.

Again, Abdul pushed forward. "What's the big deal? It's just a stupid sport—"

"Shut up, Abdul!" Rita screamed. "You do not get a say in this or anything else." She lowered her voice, fixing him with a blank, almost detached glare. "You are nothing but a criminal."

For a moment he and their mother just stared, neither wanting to be the first to look away.

Abdul spun on his heel and barged out of the yard, shouldering their dad out the way as he went. The front door opened and slammed shut.

In the silence, her mother took her hand. "I do this because it is my responsibility to keep you on the right path. It is too late for Abdul. He has made his choice. But I cannot and *will* not let you do the same."

Her mother's weighty words, and the realisation that if she was to keep on fighting, it would be without her family by her side, landed harder than any blow in the ring.

She nodded coldly, and headed inside to her room. Her father offered sympathetic eyes, but he turned away and sat back at the kitchen table.

In the full house, with her father, mother and her little twin siblings, a horrible loneliness fell upon Ila.

CHAPTER 23

Not wanting to go home, and yet feeling terrible guilt for leaving Jo and Beth to her dad's mercy, Rose had called up Petra.

Luckily Petra had pinched a bit of weed from her brother's stash, and Rose had to admit that as much as she didn't like the stuff, it had certainly taken the edge off.

They sprawled on the play equipment at the local park, Petra's head still deep into her phone as it always was, but she hadn't stopped talking.

Unlike Rose, Petra got super hyped on weed. "Holy shit!" Petra blurted. "Look at this!"

Thrusting her phone at Rose, she pointed to a video playing on the screen. It was shaky and a tad pixelated, but she recognised the school uniforms.

"Is this...?" She began to ask. But her words left her, as she watched Tierney stand from a bench and fold her arms. Then she saw herself come into frame. Rose actually winced as she watched herself rip into the girl. Then she was on top, throwing down a staggering amount of punches.

"Wait for it!" Petra said, a gleeful expression on her face.

Petra suddenly launched herself on to the back of one of Tierney's friends. "Boom!" she laughed.

Rose forced a chuckle, but took the phone from Petra and skipped back the video to the vision of her punching a helpless Tierney. The girl's head bounced between Rose's fist and the concrete of the playground.

"Shit..." she breathed.

She hadn't realised just how bad the beating she'd dished out actually was. The video played on, and Rose was dragged off the girl. The queen of the school lay motionless on the ground.

"Told you," Petra said, taking back the phone.

"Is she back at school yet?"

Petra shook her head.

"I just wanted them to stop."

"Yeah, well, not much you can do now, hey?"

A horrible, twisting guilt churned in her stomach. It had felt good to hurt the queen, but Jesus, she hadn't meant to hurt her that badly. Well, maybe she had at the time. But now...

Her thoughts wandered to the fighters at the gym, and the protection they wore when they sparred. Now she understood why.

"I just wanted them to stop," she repeated.

Petra held up a hand. "Here, I got something else on the way out tonight." Rummaging through her bag, she produced a clear plastic bottle. Rose could tell it had been a juice bottle at one point, but now it was filled with some sort of clear liquid.

Petra was grinning widely, her eye's gleam caught in the

floodlight illuminating the playground.

"What the fuck is that?" Rose asked with a frown.

Petra's smile widened even further. "Dad's homemade grappa."

Rose reached for it without hesitation. She needed something that would help her forget her dad, help her forget Tierney. Something that would just take the edge of for a little bit. She took a long drink.

Petra tried to wrestle it back from her. "Careful, you crazy bitch! You're not meant to scull it."

Rose coughed madly as the fiery liquid assaulted her throat. Then smiled as the blissful numbness of the weed, and booze began taking effect.

CHAPTER 24

Cathy's dreamless sleep was shattered, quite literally by the crash of breaking glass. She tumbled off the couch in the office and sprang to her feet.

Cracking her neck, she tried to shake the intoxication from her body. She shouldn't be drinking so much, but with things the way they were now, the gym about to go under, her home foreclosed by the bank, Cathy thought she was at least entitled to a drink or two… or three. The problem was, she'd felt entitled to a drink more and more these days. It was the only thing that blocked out the memories and the shame.

Sometimes she felt her dad watching her. She knew it was ridiculous, but she really felt his presence.

If he could see me now, she thought, really hoping he couldn't.

The dead can't judge, but you can judge yourself.

Another smash.

Grave voices and cursing emanated from the front area beyond the office. So, there was more than one junkie out there. Well, she didn't care if there were ten of them, they were going to get a good thrashing for breaking into her gym.

Adrenalin pulsed through her. Cracking her knuckles, she

threw open her office door.

Three silhouettes spun to face her. Two were rather tall and stocky, the other far shorter.

Leaping the counter, she landed with cat like grace in front of them. Although she swayed slightly, the booze still thick in her system. "You fuckers picked the wrong business to lift," she announced hotly.

"Cathy?" a voice asked out of the black.

She straightened to stare at the three figures. Cathy recognised that voice. She reached over the counter, and switched on the small light that illuminated the reception area. It was weak, but enough to reveal the intruders.

When she saw the face of the smaller man, she let out a groan of disbelief. "Ange?"

Angelo glared back at her. Apparently just as surprised to see her. "What the fuck are you doing here?" he asked.

Cathy scoffed. "Me? What the fuck, are *you* doing here?"

The man who had been her father's friend, whom she'd known since she was a little girl running around the gym and climbing the punching bags, had just broken into her business, her *home*, with two other blokes.

"Well?" she demanded, throwing up her hands.

Angelo pulled at his collar shifting with embarrassment. "Look, I thought you might be holding out on me for the money," he said with a shrug.

She shook her head in complete disbelief. "So, you're here to rob me? Is that it?"

But Angelo's face was one of concern. He took a few

hesitant steps toward her. "Cathy… you're not living here, are you? Jesus, girl, if your father was still alive to see you like this—"

"I appreciate your concern, Ange," she said, her voice oozing sarcasm. "But it doesn't really explain to me why you and these two fuckheads are standing in *my* gym in the middle of the bloody night!"

The thugs moved forward menacingly. They were solid blokes both. Cathy spotted a few tattoos on their hands, and was pretty confident it meant they were affiliated with one of the major bikie gangs. They were thugs for hire, and the fact that they were gang affiliated sent a shiver down her spine. Guys like that would do anything for money, and not lose a second of sleep over it.

Her voice betrayed her as she uttered, "I'm calling the cops!"

Angelo smiled at the quiver in her tone. "Jesus, Cathy, your dad would turn in his grave if he knew you were living like this."

All three were approaching now.

"Listen, you'll get your money, I just-"

But Angelo scoffed and held up a silencing hand. "You know, I hear that a lot, Cathy," he said. "A *lot*."

For a moment no one spoke. No one had to. She knew what was about to happen. As did they.

Their eyes were cruel, indifferent, and Cathy had seen enough violence in her life to know when it was about to explode. Eyes were a tell-all as to the type of person you were about to dance with. The two bikie's eyes had seen so much violence it was probably a daily occurrence.

Subtly she dropped her right leg back a touch, and kept her hands near her chin. The quickest way to end the fight was to take out the two big guys with some nicely timed shots to the knee or groin.

But the alcohol still burning through her system was slowing her. Despite the adrenalin pumping through her veins, Cathy knew her reaction time was desperately slower than she needed it to be.

The two thugs were poised to strike, when Angelo called out. "Wait! Everyone just wait," he said. "How much do you have right now?"

She dropped her hands, her head followed. "Three hundred... maybe four." Her voice came with that quiver again.

Angelo held out his hand. She moved around the counter, retrieved the cash from her strongbox and handed it over.

Angelo passed it to one of his cronies who tucked it away. He casually lent on the counter, the two thugs flanking him. "You call the pigs on me, and all this..." he waved a hand at the gym area, "is gone for good. My offer still stands, but not for much longer. So, no more fucking around, you understand?"

One of the Bikies lashed out grabbing hold of her hair and arm. She attempted to slip his grasp, but he was too quick and the alcohol had betrayed her agility.

He dragged her over the counter and dumped her on the floor. The two of them began stomping and kicking her repeatedly.

It was a savage, but mercifully short beating. Angelo quickly called them off.

One of the thugs scooped her up against the counter. Hanging there, with the world spinning under the harsh neon light, the vodka threatened to come back up in her throat.

"Please don't make me have to do this again," Angelo cooed. "It hurts me too much to see my old friend's daughter like this."

The thug dropped her to the ground, and she lay there coughing and squirming.

They left without a backward glance.

A car on the street started up and roared off.

The night returned to silence.

After a while she struggled up, turned off the light, and collapsed back on the couch.

When she found she couldn't sleep, she took another bottle of vodka from the cupboard in the kitchenette and drank until the sweet dreamless sleep dragged her under again.

CHAPTER 25

P etra launched an attempted hug but only succeeded in tumbling forward. They both descended into peals of laughter. The girls were well and truly drunk. The grappa had hit hard and fast, not to mention the weed they'd puffed before.

Still slumped on the play equipment, Rose gulped down another swig of the almost empty bottle while Petra continued blurting out the story she'd been telling for a good twenty minutes.

"So, I turn around, and he's standing there naked, with this look on his face like…" She did her best caveman voice, "'We fuck now?'"

Rose couldn't hold in the laughter and spat half of her drink across the play equipment.

"I look down…" Petra continued through her laughter, "and all I can see is this little twig poking out of this bush of pubes! I've never seen such a tiny dick!"

"What did you say?" she managed between snorts of laughter.

"Hey little fella, does Mummy know you're out late?"

Their howls echoed around the park. Slowly however, the laughter subsided, and the pair leant drunkenly against each other.

Petra lay back, her head resting on Rose's knee. Dark hair swept to one side. She closed her eyes, a contented smile slipping across her lips.

Rose found herself staring down at her friend in a strange drunken clarity. All the unsettling, yet oddly pleasant feelings she'd been having about her friend became clear in that moment.

"Boys are so fucked," Petra giggled, her eyes still shut, the smile still on her lips.

Rose took another sip from the bottle. It was painfully clear to her now. And she didn't know what to do.

She loved Petra.

But not that platonic love someone feels for a friend when they're a few drinks in. She loved this girl, deeper than she'd ever realised.

"P…?" she started, but stopped immediately. She had no idea what to say.

"Hmm?" Petra hummed sleepily.

What should she say? Should she say anything? What would Petra think? Before Rose could really ponder any of these questions, she found herself leaning forward, sweeping Petra's dark hair from her cheek and kissing her softly on the lips.

It was only a heartbeat of a moment, but for Rose it felt like an eternity. A moment trapped in a lifetime.

Petra's eyes flew open. She shoved Rose roughly away and jerked up to standing. Instantly, she was sober. "What are you doing?" she demanded.

Rose's heart sank as reality hit. Petra's face was a mix of confusion, anger and...fear?

"P... I'm sorry... I..."

"Why the fuck did you do that?"

"I'm sorry... I don't know...P, I didn't mean..." She reached out, but Petra pushed her away.

Her friend flashed Rose a glare of betrayal, grabbed her bag and bolted from the park.

Rose's head dropped into her hands. Had she just lost her only friend in the world? What did she think would happen? That Petra would suddenly throw her arms around Rose and reciprocate? Who was she to suddenly, and without warning, force herself on a girl who had always thought of her as a friend? Nothing more than that. And yet Rose had just laid a kiss on Petra from seemingly out of nowhere.

Pressing her face harder into her hands, Rose screamed. The muffled sound bounced around the empty, and now very cold park.

She snatched up the discarded bottle and drained the remains of the burning liquid.

Rose was more alone than ever now.

CHAPTER 26

Night still blanketed the sky, but the first rays of day crept over the horizon. Cathy lurched from the couch, the vodka bottle tipped at her feet. She snatched it up before too much of the precious liquid was lost.

Tipping it down her throat, she almost laughed at how pathetic she must look as it spilled down the side of her face. What was there to care about now? There was nothing left for her. She could only wait until Angelo returned with his bikie mates.

Life had always been a challenge of survival, and she had survived much of what had been thrown at her. Relationship breakdowns, her dad's passing, her bank account running dry. Those were just some of the highlights. Again, she felt the melancholic urge to laugh at herself but it only manifested tears.

This gym was all she had left of her life, and that was about to be ripped from her too.

Cathy stood, fell to her knees, and struggled up again. She felt like a fighter after copping a kick to the side of the head.

Those were the days. Things were so much easier in the

ring. Your problems stood right in front of you and threw punches. But at least they were tangible, and you could fight back.

She caught her reflection glaring at her in the office window. "The fuck you looking at?"

The woman in the window continued to glare back. She brought her hands up into fists. She slipped and weaved and punched and kicked at the air. But she couldn't hit the woman in the window, and the woman couldn't hit her.

What was it she'd said to the kid? *'You can't just go around punching your problems in the face.'*

Letting out a despairing grunt, she kicked her desk and slumped into the chair. The photo of her with her dad toppled forward. The contents of her stomach were about to come flying back up.

Her dad couldn't bear to see her like this, but she reached over and righted the photo. Duncan White looked up at his daughter with his endearing smile.

"Sorry, Dad… I tried."

Dawn finally broke, and Cathy broke with it, tears streaming down her face yet to Cathy it felt like she was laughing at a great joke that life had played on her.

Hope. That was the joke. Life pretended to give me hope.

CHAPTER 27

No matter which way Rose angled her face; the sun found a way to assault her eyes. This hangover was bad, but she'd definitely had worse. Her thoughts were a mess – regretful and frustrated. Every time she thought about the kiss, her heart ached. At least she assumed that's what it was. She couldn't think of any other way to articulate the feeling.

And she'd just freaked out her friend… No, freaked out the person she loved. Her action had just isolated the one person in this fucked-up world who had her back.

Fuck!

Pulling her phone out, she tried to concentrate on the screen through her pounding headache. *I'm never fucking drinking again! Ever!*

She texted Petra, it was about the tenth time she'd tried her this morning. 'Please can I just talk to you?'

Rose hit send. After a beat the word, 'seen', appeared next to the message. But no response was forthcoming.

Arriving at the gym, she stuffed the phone away, and stopped dead. Glass covered the front area. The inside of the gym was pitch black. She cast a wary look up and down the street, but as always, the industrial street was empty.

Sticking her head through the bottom section of the glass door, being careful to avoid the shards hanging from the frame, she called into the empty space. Her voice bounced around the cavernous gym. With even more caution, she ducked inside.

"Hello?" Movement in the office caught her attention, and Rose hurried forward, her hangover forgotten.

Barging her way into the office, fists raised, heart pumping, she came across Cathy sprawled on the couch. Rose dropped her fists when she saw the empty bottle beside the woman. The grizzled coach still had her red bandana on. Strangely, it occurred to Rose that in the week or so that she'd been here, she'd never seen Cathy without it wrapped around her head.

"You're late," came a dull groan from the couch. Cathy's eyes flickered open, bloodshot and the same colour as her bandana.

"What happened?" Rose asked.

Cathy struggled to sitting, her head drooping heavily. "Nothing you need to worry about," she said.

As Cathy forced herself to stand, swaying slightly as she did, Rose spotted a nasty bruise under her eye. "You walk into a door?" she asked.

Cathy shot Rose a grim smile. "Touché." Moving over to the kitchenette, she flicked the kettle on and snatched a filthy mug from the sink.

Rose didn't want to think about how long that mug had probably sat there.

"Head home, kid," Cathy croaked. "I'm not opening

today."

"Could I still train?" Rose asked. "I don't mind doing it on my own."

The old coach let out a long, pained breath as the kettle whistled, matching her tone. Pouring coffee as she spoke, her voice lacked the fiery energy that Rose had seen in the woman. "Listen, and *actually* listen, don't just hear that I'm talking and tune it out," she said. "I know what kids are like."

She turned to face Rose. In her bloodshot eyes, there was a cold, unforgiving truth. "Being a fighter? It's not what you want. Trust me. It looks good in movies and all that shit. But the reality?" she gestured to the office and herself. "It's something much different. Besides, I've got a few other things on my mind."

"I know!" Rose protested. "I just want to train, that's all."

"Why?" Cathy leant against the sink, her face cold, impassive.

Rose had the feeling that her next words had better be convincing. "When I watch them... the fighters you train I mean, when they're in the ring it's like nothing else matters." She searched desperately for the words; suddenly wishing she'd paid attention in English literature class.

"It's almost like they're at peace—"

Cathy barked a cruel laugh, almost spilling her coffee. "Are you fucking serious? You think getting punched in the face brings you peace?"

"That's not what I meant," Rose retorted hotly.

Cathy raised a calming hand but the anger was flaming

inside Rose. However, another part of her mind switched on, gently reminding her that this woman, old though she may be, still had four black belts hanging in the locker, and more experience fighting than Rose had days on the earth.

The rage was quickly smothered.

"My dad started this place for little shits like you," Cathy said, her eyes firmly on the picture sitting on her desk. "The idea was to get them off the drugs, the drink, give them something to strive for." She nodded to the gym area. "And it worked. I know because…" her eyes locked on Rose. "I was one of those little shits."

Those eyes held Rose for a long, sobering moment, and Rose could feel the years of experience and battles Cathy had fought.

"I've been doing my running," Rose offered meekly.

"And drinking too, by the smell of you."

Rose nodded to the empty bottle on the floor.

Cathy snorted. "Yeah, fair point." The older lady rubbed her forehead and closed her eyes for a moment. Rose knew a decision was coming. "If you miss *one* training session," she said forcefully. "You're done! I call David and tell him you've dropped out."

Rose felt her face light up. "I can train? Like… properly?"

Cathy nodded. "But you're not fighting in any comps or any of that shit! And if you use any of what you learn out there on the street or in school, I'll knock you out myself! Got it?"

Rose couldn't control her smile; she was going to get

to train! Just like the fighters she'd watched the other day. "Thank you," she said earnestly.

"No worries. Lesson one, how to empty the bins properly!"

CHAPTER 28

Cathy downed another strong coffee, and soon the pounding in her head started to fade. She watched as the kid swept up the glass in the entranceway, then carefully tipped the shards into the bin. She didn't need a psychology degree to understand this kid had been through a lot, and she'd lost count of the number of troubled teens, homeless kids, and just general no-hopers that had come through the gym when her dad was alive.

She'd tried to keep the program going, but honestly, she just didn't have the same passion as her father. Cathy had simply wanted to run a gym and make some real money. She had done just that, for a time at least. But when the businesses in the area started to shut down and the locals moved away, the clients simply dropped off.

Now the kid was trying to patch the broken window with ply-board. Cathy moved to give her a hand.

Most of the people who said they wanted to train and become fighters didn't last. The dedication to get up early, train hard, eat like a monk and be able to do it consistently usually got the better of them.

Not to mention the first time they caught a proper punch to the face. She grinned darkly at the thought. *That always rocks their world.*

Sure, the kid was tough, but it would remain to be seen if she was resilient too.

"Leave that." Cathy said. She moved toward the ring and snatched up a pair of crusty boxing gloves from under the canvas and tossed them to Rose. "Get in the ring. It's time."

la was sure she was going to pass out. The heat of the afternoon mixed with the stuffy confines of the cavernous community hall sent rivers of sweat down her face. She'd drunk about two litres of water and hadn't gone to the toilet yet. The thought amused her, and she let out a chuckle.

"What the hell are you laughing about?"

She snapped around to face Michael. He was dressed in jeans and a T-shirt with the gym's logo on it. Taking in the spacious change room around her, reality suddenly slapped her across the face.

Fight day was finally here.

She was going to step into the octagon cage in front of a paying audience and attempt to knock another girl out.

Her smile quickly departed.

This was real.

It was happening right now.

While she sat in stillness, her blood pulsed with the fury of a tempest.

"That's the way, girl!" Michael called as he slipped on some focus pads. "Wipe that stupid grin off your face and at least act hard."

Dressed in shorts, and a sports top, which showed a lot of her stomach, Ila shifted nervously. She'd never worn anything so revealing before, even in training. There was no way her mum would let her be seen in public like this.

But she wasn't here, thank God.

The echo of limbs cracking off pads, not to mention the burning waft of Deep Heat cream in the air, was getting a little overwhelming. The tempest was still raging within and showed no sign of easing.

"Hey," he said moving closer. She found his smell of cheap deodorant surprisingly comforting in its familiarity. "You good?"

"No."

"Come on, don't tell me you're letting this lot get to you?" he said with a nod to the other fighters warming up.

"Which girl am I fighting again?"

"I told you before, don't worry about her!"

She let out a strained breath and tried to give him a confident look, but his expression told her the attempt had failed horribly.

Slapping his focus pads together, he waved her forward. "Just focus on the game plan and what *you* need to do. Don't let emotions get the better of you. Now give me some kicks!"

Working simple combos, jabs, front kicks, and her takedowns, her mind calmed as she lost herself in the repetition of the strikes. The tempest became a focused energy. It felt good. It felt right.

"Ila Abara! And Emily Parker!" a voice hollered from the entrance of the change rooms.

Michael threw his pads aside. "Here we go. You ready?"

She was, and it only took a glance from him to see it.

He led her out into the hall.

The official who'd called their names waved them to a stop just outside the change room.

He was a burly man, but potbellied, the heat causing him to sweat waves down his pudgy cheeks. She took in the large hall. The octagon cage stood proudly in the centre. Several people scattered about the place made up the audience. This was clearly no pay-per-view event.

Some of the people noticed her waiting in the wings, but none seemed overly interested.

Becoming aware of someone beside her, she turned to see a woman about her own age also dressed in fight gear. She gave Ila a nod as she loosened up. The woman had long blonde hair plaited into a braid. It gave her the look of an ancient Celtic warrior.

"Good luck, ay!" the girl bellowed in a broad Aussie accent.

This was her opponent? She sounded like a typical rough-neck. Hard as rusted nails, and Ila had the feeling this girl was used to getting into scraps. Probably did it for a laugh.

"Just take it to the ground and she's done," Michael whispered in her ear.

The official waved them forward. "All right, head to the cage. Good luck, ladies!"

As they made their way down, the small crowd seemed to

gain some interest.

A ring announcer stepped into the cage with them while Michael moved to his position outside the cage, as did Emily's trainer.

"Fight two in the Novice Featherweight division. Fighting out of the red corner, representing Redburn MMA with a record of one win and no losses – Emily Parker," said the announcer into a microphone, which screeched with feedback.

The audience cringed and groaned.

Emily raised her hand to the crowd, who clapped politely.

"And her opponent, on debut, fighting out of Atlas Brazilian Jiu Jitsu, Ila Abara!"

The referee called the two of them to the centre of the cage. Despite all her efforts to control her nerves, her heart smashed against her ribs at a furious pace.

"Ok, ladies, we've been over the rules in the dressing room, follow my instructions at all times. Now touch gloves and come out fighting."

They bumped gloves. Emily's knuckles felt like rocks through the padding.

Ila could feel the tempest pulsing through her body as she walked back to her corner.

You've got this! This is what you've trained for.

Michael was instructing her through the cage, and she tried to concentrate. What was he saying?

"…keep moving and look for the takedowns. Do not get into a punch-on with this girl."

"Why? You said she's only had one fight."

Michael looked sheepishly at her. "Yeah… Well, she's only had one MMA fight. She's had about fifteen kickboxing bouts."

"You tell me this now?" she hissed in disbelief.

"Listen! This is why I agreed to the fight, she's got no submission or takedown game. So, what do we do?"

Ila nodded. "Take her to the ground."

Facing Emily, who bounced lightly on her feet, Ila could almost read her thoughts in those eyes. This girl was itching for that bell to sound.

The referee was pointing at her. "You ready?"

No. "Yes!"

He asked the same of Emily, who simply nodded.

Ding!

"Fight!" the referee yelled gruffly.

Emily came at her like an avalanche of limbs.

"Shit," Ila whispered.

The first punch from Emily sent her reeling. The follow up shot landed square on her jaw with a shock of agony. There was no head guard to absorb the power of the strike.

Her knees buckled. Emily threw consecutive front kicks, each one stung like a whip across her flesh.

The blows continued to land as she crashed against the cage. "Cover up!" Michael screamed. But the blows kept landing.

The referee was suddenly beside them as Emily clinched her against the cage and tried to line up a knee strike.

"Defend, or I'm stopping the fight!" the referee yelled at her.

Emily released her and threw a devastating elbow, catching Ila right on the chin.

Her head bounced off the cage, and the world spun but the blow had a strange effect. The strike seemed to whip her head into a sense of clarity.

The tempest surged.

Pushing off the cage, Ila moved laterally away. Emily followed, stalking her with her strikes and cutting off the cage for her escape.

But Ila's adrenalin was pumping, and she knew she'd be in trouble if Emily landed any more blows.

Fighting back with some of her own combinations, she burned with frustration as Emily simply slipped out the way or blocked the punches.

"Take down, Ila! Take down!" Michael screamed, slapping his hand on the canvas.

She slipped forward, attempting to grab Emily for a hip toss but the woman caught her in a clinch, her hands around the back of her neck, and threw staggeringly powerful knees. The breath was driven out of her as she was struck below the ribs.

Instinctively, Ila snatched up Emily's leg before another knee-strike could land. Lifting the leg high, she drove her weight down. Emily lost balance and went crashing to the mat.

"Yes!" Michael yelled with surprise. "Wear her down, Ila! Don't go for mount yet!"

But she did.

She flattened Emily on her back and finally got some

punches in. Bringing her fist down like a hammer.

Emily could not escape from beneath her. "Go for the submission!" She heard Michael call.

Gaining the top position, she caught Emily's arm and twisted. Their eyes locked, Emily tried to resist the submission, and hold on until the end of the round but Ila twisted the arm back further.

A defeated, pleading look came into Emily's eyes. The Celtic warrior was beaten, and she knew it.

Ila twisted that little bit more, and Emily slapped the mat with her free hand. The referee pulled her off her opponent.

Emily had tapped out!

Ila flopped on her back in the centre of the cage. The rush of her inner tempest was fading fast, the pain from the dozens of punches, kicks, and knees she'd taken returned to her body like a flood.

Michael was suddenly there grinning down at her.

"I won," she stated in surprise.

He laughed. "You did!"

He yanked her to standing, and Emily came over and shook her hand, congratulating her in that rough Aussie drawl. The referee then raised Ila's hand in victory.

Again, came some polite clapping from the small, mildly interested crowd.

They were bustled out of the cage, inspected by the doctor and then Ila was given a small plastic trophy.

The rest of the afternoon was a blur.

After she'd had a shower and cleaned up, Michael drove

her home talking excitedly about the fight. Picking at every detail and move. He kept talking all the way back to her house.

She asked to be dropped a few streets over from the flats, and when he asked why, she lied, saying she needed to see a friend.

They talked a bit longer, but she wasn't taking in much of the conversation.

He hugged her goodbye, and she hopped out into the empty street under the huge building.

Once his car was out of sight, Ila keeled over and vomited.

The thousand eyes of the building watched on, impassive as ever.

CHAPTER 30

U ntil night fell, Ila stood opposite her house, running her fingers over the bumps and bruises coating her face. When the streetlights blinked on, she knew it was time to walk across to the house and confront her mum.

Ila was not a little girl anymore, but she still dreaded the repercussions, even if she was resigned to them.

It's my life, and my choice. She kept up that mantra all the way to her home, right up to the front door. Before she could even retrieve her keys, the door creaked open. Her mother's face appeared, eyes grave and unforgiving.

Silently they regarded each other, Ila wondering how long her mother had watched her loitering across the road.

"Where have you been," her mother asked.

Ila retrieved the trophy from her bag, offering it up to her. "I won this."

Her mother reached out, gripped Ila's chin, and inspected the state of her daughter's face.

"Mum... I..."

Her mother released her, and abruptly closed the door without another word. The deadlock slid across, and the porch light went out.

Ila tossed the trophy back into her bag and moved off down the street. Her dreams were bright, but the path she walked to reach them was turning as dark and lonely as the night around her.

*

It was unusually frosty in Michael's gym, but still warmer than the reception she'd got at home. Ila had run a few classes for Michael a few weeks back when he was sick, and still had a key.

Double-checking that she'd locked the door, she moved through to the training area, thankful for the dark and the silence. A throbbing in her head was growing worse by the minute. All she wished was to lie in the quiet blackness and calm her mind.

The day had been a storm of action and emotions. She'd give anything to be at home lying in her own bed, listening to the twins playing and laughing.

Even the muffled thump of Abby's music would have been a comfort.

But the silence of the gym would have to do.

She found a blanket in the office. Made a pillow out of her jacket and lay there, thoughts and hopes swirling for her attention.

Sleeping alone on the floor of the gym was not how she'd envisioned the aftermath of her first victory. Two conflicts were pulling at her. One tugged in the direction of the fight inside the cage, the other pulled in the direction of the fight outside the cage.

Life.

CHAPTER 31

F eet slapping the pavement in a solid rhythm, Rose cast her eyes to the sun stretching into the pale morning sky. Every day for about a week now, she'd been running at the crack of dawn. Focusing on what she had to do in the moment rather than what may or may not happen in the future was strengthening her mind. Cutting out the anger and fear.

Focus on this moment right now. All you have to do is run.

Nothing else mattered. And really, she didn't have anything else now. No Petra, no school, nothing.

When she had told Cathy she was doing morning runs, the coach had smiled dangerously and said, "Good. Now we'll have more time to get you working the bag and the pads."

And work her Cathy had. Rose could hardly walk by the end of each day. Especially since Cathy still forced her to complete all her cleaning as well as assist her when she was training the fighters.

Slowing to a walk, hands on hips, she sucked in deep breaths of morning air. Pushing through the side gate, she entered the house through the back door. Jo almost jumped out of her skin when she stepped into the kitchen.

Rose's face contorted into a mask of concern. Jo's eyes still bore purple and black bruises from that night. She'd made an attempt to cover them with concealer, but that seemed to make them stand out even more.

"Have you been out all night?" she asked in a hushed, but still forceful tone. "If you're dad finds out you've been partying—"

"Relax, I've been out for a run. I've been every morning this week."

Jo's hands went to her hips, and her face switched to a mask of skepticism, "Bullshit."

"If I do my run early, I have more time to do my technique training during the day."

"Training?" Jo was still squinting at her in suspicion. "When you were going to school, you'd stumble out of bed, grunt a hello and then fuck off to catch the bus."

"Yeah, well, I'm not at school now."

Jo's gaze softened, and she gestured to the kitchen table. "You want something to eat? I'm about to do breakfast."

"Nah, it's all good." Rose whipped opened the fridge, retrieving a plate. "I made this last night. There's enough for you and Beth too."

Jo stopped her with a touch. "Are you all right, love?"

Rose laughed at her step-mum's bewilderment.

"Jesus, I don't think I've heard you laugh... ever," Jo said.

The pair of them shared a wistful smile. In that brief moment, she felt a connection to Jo she hadn't felt with anyone. Not since her mother was alive.

The moment passed as the patter of tiny feet sprinted down the hall and into the kitchen. Beth leapt into her arms, and Rose had the feeling it was Beth who was really embracing her, and not the other way around.

She looked to Jo. "Where is he?"

Taking Beth and sitting the child on her lap, Jo sighed. "He isn't home yet, love. Went out with some mates last night.

You know how it is," she said, feeding Beth as she spoke.

"What is this?" Jo asked.

"Something called, Granola," Rose said. "I read it's good for you. I added the fruit, and acai berries before I left. You let it soak and the milk absorbs all the healthy shit." She made a face and shrugged. "At least that's what Google said."

"Well, it's better than toast and eggs for the ten thousandth time," Jo said. She reached out and gave Rose's hand a squeeze.

As she leant over, Beth looked up at her mother, reaching a hand to touch one of the bruises dotting Jo's cheek.

Rose took the opportunity to address the one problem they all shared. But Jo seemed to read her mind before she even spoke.

"Not in front of Beth."

But Rose's anger was building, the old rage swelling back to the surface. She wasn't angry with Jo, just fed up at the situation they were in. "Why don't we call your parents," she offered desperately. "Didn't they say they'd take us in—"

"Leave it, Rosie," Jo said. "I really don't want to talk about it now."

But she pressed on. "Cathy, the woman who runs the

gym, she says we don't have to put up with it! She says shit is different these days—"

Jo threw her spoon down to clatter across the table, startling both Rose and Beth.

"Cathy says? Who's Cathy? What the fuck does she know about it? Does she have two kids to look after? Does she have to go and wait in fucking Centrelink for two hours at a fucking time just to get seven hundred and seventy-six bucks a fucking fortnight? What would this Cathy do? Call the pigs? You of all people know how well that shit works." She ran a hand through her stringy hair. Her eyes went down to Beth, and her words seemed more to herself than for Rose. "They all just want to get their pay cheques, none of them give a shit. Never have."

But Rose refused to let it go. Her dad was a ticking bomb with a short fuse, and she wasn't blind to the way he looked at her sometimes, and she'd felt the way he touched her. He was looking at her as if she belonged to him, as if he had the right to… to want something from her. Something that terrified her more than anything.

It made her sick, but worse, it made her feel like nothing, just an object.

"Listen!" Rose pressed, her fury rising and her tone firm, but she was careful not to lose control. "Maybe if we go to the cops together—"

"No! I don't trust those fuckers! All they do is—"

The clunk of the front door unlocking sent them both silent. Jo pushed Beth toward Rose, and she took the child protectively in her arms. Jo hurried to busy herself at the kitchen sink.

Her father entered; eyes red, hair a mess and the familiar smell of bourbon and coke permeating his pours. "Am I interrupting something?"

Rose couldn't look at him, but luckily it was Jo who did the heavy lifting. "Morning, love! Here, sit down and try this. Rosie made it." She nodded to the bowl on the table. "How was your night?"

He gave a thin smile and plonked himself down. "Yeah, a big one. Sorry I didn't come home, but I thought it would be safer to stay at Johno's place. Bloody pigs everywhere on the roads these days."

He ate a spoonful, raising surprised eyes to Rose. "This is bloody good! You made this?"

Jo beamed proudly. "And she's been out running."

"No shit? Ah! I see what's going on, they got you training down there, hey? Gonna learn to throw a few proper punches?"

He slapped the table and laughed warmly. "Nah, that's great! Be good for you to learn a bit a discipline. Just what you need young lady."

She didn't want to leave Jo and Beth alone with him, but what could she do? Unless Jo was on-board, they would live forever in fear of this man and his emotional violence.

"I need to go," she stated bluntly. Standing quickly and placing Beth in her chair, she headed for the hallway. He caught her hand.

"Rosie... I just... Look, I'm sorry about the other night. You know how I get when there's no work on and the stress, it just gets to me. Look, I just want to say I'm sorry, and thank you for this." He gestured to the food.

She flashed her eyes to Jo, who raised an eyebrow in return.

Rose cringed, because just like that, it seemed to her Jo was back under his spell. He always said the right things when it mattered.

She nodded. "You're welcome."

"Now go get 'em, beautiful!"

His hand found its way to her backside. Her whole body clenched as he softly patted her, his hand resting there for a moment.

Slipping out of his touch, she grabbed her bag and left without another word.

CHAPTER 32

The day was creeping to an end by the time Cathy put Rose through her training.

Because she'd bolted from the house in such a hurry that morning, she'd not eaten, nor had she packed any lunch. Her stomach was loudly protesting the lack of food and as a result, a savage headache was building behind her eyes. But she threw on her gloves and stepped into the ring where Cathy stood with focus pads on her hands and shin guards on her legs.

The greying coach pushed Rose to the absolute limits of endurance. Kicks and punches flew, but Cathy would occasionally throw punches back, albeit half-heartedly, and she constantly yelled at Rose to, "Keep your bloody hands up!"

Finally, Rose slumped in the corner of the ring, her lungs craving more air than they could take in.

Cathy whipped off her bandana and wiped her dripping face. Ringing out the sweat on to the mat as she talked. "You're doing well, kid. I can tell you're motivated right now, and that's good. But the test is how strong can you build your mind? Right now you must be here, but tell me, what happens when you aren't? Can you still drag your ass out of bed early to go running? Then head off to school or work, then head back into training and do that over and over? You got heart, but hearts get broken easily when the real struggle comes. So, keep showing me a strong mind, and I'll keep working with you."

Grabbing Rose's wrist, she hoisted her back to her feet. "Now, get cleaned up, you stink," she said. "Oh, and clean up this sweat patch you made." She flashed a wicked smile, and tied her bandana back up as she slipped out of the ring.

Rose had to laugh, this was all a test, and it was a test she felt she was winning.

She headed for the showers, her mind clear and calm.

This was the peace she'd sought. This was the path she wanted.

But it was long, and there was still much to do.

CHAPTER 33

L adies! How are we?"

Rose looked up from her mopping, and Cathy almost snapped the pen she was holding as Angelo sauntered toward them.

He paused to stamp the dirt from his shoes onto the area she'd just mopped.

Cathy folded her arms. Her muscles tensed like springs, and Rose noticed a vein at her temple was pulsing madly. "You got some nerve, Ange," she grunted.

But he simply smiled his smug smile, adjusted his suit collar and held out his hand.

Cathy's stoicism faded. Opening the cash register, she emptied the few notes. He took them without a word, strolled casually toward the front door, and stuffed a twenty-dollar bill down Rose's T-shirt.

She glared up at him, the fire of rage beginning to ignite. But he'd already turned back to Cathy. "Oh, by the way, Bomber, my previous offer? It's off the table. Everything you owe me by the end of the month or I *will* take this instead." He gestured to the gym. "Of course, you'll see me before then."

He left without another word.

Rose swung around to Cathy, her face hot with anger. But seeing her coach's eyes, she understood it was best to stay silent. She fished the note out of her top, and placed it on the counter in front of Cathy. After a beat, Cathy snatched it up and shoved it back in the cash register.

It seemed there was a major obstacle in Rose's new path. One she had no idea how to combat. If there was no gym, there would be no training.

When she left for the night, she passed the office window. Cathy was sitting at her desk contemplating the unopened bottle of vodka in front of her.

Rose hoped the bloody thing would stay that way, but it was unlikely.

CHAPTER 34

The fact that Marley's car was worth about half the value of the car's stereo was a continual source of amusement to Abdul. The beats spewing from the audio system assaulted the street, but no one would dare come out and complain. Not while he and the boys hung there, smoking and just generally being rowdy.

Every now and then a fearful face peered out from behind a curtain, but it was quickly withdrawn.

The boys were up for a big night it seemed, and while he'd been feeling a little reserved about going out recently, it only took a few drinks to change his mind. However, he'd begged the boys not to start shit tonight. He'd had enough of throwing down for a while.

They had shrugged and nodded. But Abdul had a nagging feeling that trouble was still around the corner. He did his best to brush it off, and Marley passing him a fresh joint helped.

"Should we hit up the city tonight?" he asked the group.

"I don't care where we go, as long as there's drinks and bitches," one of the boys announced to the whole street. There was a short spout of laughter, then Aaron, one of his more tubby friends gestured down the street.

"Speaking of," he wheezed. "Who is... *that*?"

They turned as one to look in the same direction.

Ila was approaching. She was still dressed in her training gear, shorts and a tight singlet, her bag slung over her shoulder. If their mum caught her wearing that, she'd cop a hell of an ear full.

"That's my sister you fat fuck," he hissed over his shoulder.

"Well shit bro, she didn't get her looks from your side of the family, that's for sure," Marley whispered.

"Any of you even think about what I *know* you're thinking about, and I'll put your head through that fucking window," he said, and nodded to the car.

The boys giggled like school kids laughing at a dirty joke. Abdul walked over to meet her. The last thing he wanted to think about was his friends mentally undressing his sister.

She offered him a genuine but fatigued smile, rubbing at the bruise under her eye.

"Shit, girl, look at your face! You sure you won that fight?"

She gave a sniff of a laugh. "Could you do something for me?"

"Where were you last night? Stay with your white boy?" he asked, unable to keep the aggression out of his voice.

But she ignored him... or was too tied to argue. Her voice soft but direct. "Can you grab my Uni books and my other training gear? It's all on my bed." She held out her bag.

A horrible fear suddenly fell over him. He was losing his sister. She wasn't playing their mother's game anymore. The girl, whose life had been planned out for her, was now guiding herself.

"Please?" she pressed. He realised he was lost in his thoughts. Taking the bag from her with a nod, he headed inside. He saw Ila glance at the boys. They all suddenly spun their gaze from her to anywhere else.

At least his warning had got through to those idiots.

He was in and out of the house as quickly as possible. Luckily their mother was hanging out the washing, and the twins were transfixed by the television.

And their dad was probably sulking in his room. He shook his head at the thought. What kind of man checked out of life like that?

He would never be that weak.

Ila was waiting, and the boys were still subtly ogling her. Again, they flipped their gaze to anywhere else on the street.

"Here," he said.

She took the bag. "Thanks, Abby."

"Hey, I heard there was a cold snap coming. Take this too." He pulled off his hoodie and handed it to her. "You know how fucking icy it gets. Africans weren't built for Melbourne!" he said.

She chuckled briefly. But it was clearly forced; her thoughts were elsewhere.

"When are you coming home? The twins miss you."

Her face dropped and she looked to their home with a mix of longing, but also an acceptance that maybe she wasn't coming back any time soon. "I don't know," she said simply.

Her gaze went from him to his four friends who were piling into Marley's ridiculously small car.

"Look after yourself, Abby," she said, and headed back the way she'd come.

He was about to call after her when one of the boys beckoned him over.

Don't think about her, she's made her choice.

"Abdul!"

He turned to the broken voice. His dad was waddling out to him, his eyes fixed wearily on the car packed with his friends.

"I'm just going to a movie with the boys, I'll be home later."

His father shielded his eyes against the late afternoon sun. "Was that your sister? Where is she going?"

"Anywhere but here," he muttered.

"Abdul, I must talk with you?" he begged.

He looked back to the car. "Later, I gotta go." He made to turn away, but his father grasped his arm desperately.

"Abdul, please... be with your family tonight," the old man implored.

He ripped his arm away roughly. "What family?"

Turning his back on his father, he climbed in the car, took the bottle of bourbon that was offered. He caught his father's pathetic outline in the side mirror. He drank until the booze stung, and passed the bottle back.

"Big night tonight boys!" he yelled, and his friends cheered. Abdul felt the addictive rush of power again. *No one can fuck with me.*

CHAPTER 35

D espite the way the afternoon had dragged, Rose's excitement was rapidly growing. The crew who had come down to spar previously were on their way over. She'd never worked so fast in her life, and even Cathy, who was never impressed with anything it seemed, gave her a physical pat on the back. Then shoved her toward the matted area and out of the way.

"You can watch, but keep quiet," she ordered.

Rose nodded and half-heartedly shadow sparred facing the mirror as the crew from the other gym arrived.

After a twenty-minute warm up, Cathy spoke to the other coach, Michael, and agreed they'd spar MMA rules. Whatever the hell that meant.

Then it was on.

Michael's fighters were much stronger when the fight went to the ground, but Cathy's fighters had superior striking.

Lost in awe at the sparring she was seeing, Rose began to feel very vulnerable around these real fighters. She'd always considered herself pretty tough. Well, physically at least. But watching the focus and calm of these guys as their opponent tried to smash their faces in, forced her to realise a truth.

There was one hell of a journey ahead of her, both mentally and physically. The door to the gym flew open. The African girl she'd spoken to last time jogged in. Michael tapped his wrist, "What time do you call this?"

Mouthing an apology, she hurried into the change room.

Two other girls had been going at an intense pace, and when the bell sounded to end their fourth-consecutive round, both dropped to their knees in exhaustion.

The African girl emerged from the change rooms, slipping on her shin pads as she made her way to the ring.

"Oi, Mike!" Cathy yelled. "Your superstar ready yet? We've been waiting for a while now."

"Yeah all right, keep your shirt on, Cath, give her a second." He turned to the girl. "Ila, go have a skip and a warm-up. Cathy! Let's give these two one more round while she warms up."

The two fighters groaned in disbelief. Neither looked overly enthusiastic about another round.

Suddenly Cathy wheeled around and fixed her sunken eyes on Rose, who stared back like a koala caught in headlights.

"What?" Rose asked, already having a worrying idea about her coach's thinking.

"Come here," Cathy said.

Rose obeyed.

"You got that mouth guard?"

"Yeah, but it's pretty shit. Keeps popping out."

Cathy bit her lip in thought, hands twisting the ring ropes. "Go and grab some shin pads and the ten-ounce MMA gloves over there." She pointed at a stack of equipment in the corner.

Cathy nodded to Michael. "We're on, mate! Get your girl in the ring."

"You cannot be serious?" Rose hissed as she returned with the pads, and Cathy guided her into the ring.

"Relax, kid, she'll go easy on you."

Michael lent over the ropes. His bright eyes flicked between them with suspicion. "You're not trying to pull a fast one, are you Cath?"

"Just a few warm-up rounds for your girl, that's all," she replied. "Now Ila, go easy, the kid is new to this."

Rose's heart rate was climbing rapidly. "What the fuck am I doing in here?" she whispered nervously. "She'll destroy me!"

Cathy slapped a head guard on her. "Calm down, its sparring, not fighting. Now, this girl will take you to the ground. When she does, and she starts hurting you, remember to tap out or chances are she'll break your arm."

She slipped Rose's mouth guard in, and slapped her on the shoulder. "Good luck, kid."

Composing herself with a shallow breath, Rose tried her best not to simply launch out of the ring and sprint through the front door. This couldn't be any worse than dealing with her dad.

Rose braced herself, moved forward, and touched gloves with Ila.

The bell sounded and the pair began circling. Her focus was centred on this girl in front of her. And in that moment, she discovered the calmness of mind she'd been searching for. She wasn't thinking of the friend she'd lost, her father, or Jo and Beth. The girls from school were a distant memory.

All that mattered was this moment.

Then Ila punched her in the face, and everything changed. Staggering back on to the ropes, she shot an alarmed glance at Cathy. The coach shook her head. "Keep... your... fucking... hands... UP!"

Rose headed back into the fray.

Ila moved with light, graceful steps, whereas Rose felt she moved with all the grace of a person in concrete shoes.

Rose began to pop her jab out, and while it didn't land, she noted it kept the taller girl at bay.

"Good!" Cathy called. "Follow the jab with your combos!"

Doing as instructed, she was promptly answered by lightning-fast strikes from Ila. Twice Ila caught her with some solid kicks to the legs, but Rose worked her defence and fired back at the taller girl.

It seemed that Ila was done playing around, and she threw a barrage of punches. But Rose covered up, and fired back a straight front kick. The strike caught her adversary square in the stomach, sending her reeling against the ropes.

"Shit, sorry!" Rose said quickly.

Cathy clutched at her bandana angrily, "Dam it, kid, it's sparring. Don't apologise!"

Ila just smiled, nodding her appreciation for the kick. Then she moved in, slid forward on one knee, caught Rose around the legs and drove her into the canvas. She had no answer to Ila's wrestling or Jiu... whatever the hell it was called. Soon she had the taller and much stronger girl lying across her, one of her arms pinned above her head. Ila wrapped an arm around her neck and squeezed.

White blotches danced in Rose's vision, and she frantically tapped out.

Ila released her and she tried to get up.

But Ila gently pushed her back down. "Breath for a second. Get your head back."

Rose did what she was told.

"That was a good round. You've got a hell of a kick on you." She helped her up and Rose was happy to see the briefest suggestion of a smile on Cathy's lips.

"Right!" Cathy yelled. "Start from standing and go again!"

Rose flashed her a glare of disbelief. Surely that was enough for one day!

Cathy folded her bulging arms. "Its either this or cleaning the bins."

Rose adjusted her head guard, then faced up to Ila again.

This was going to be a long, and painful afternoon.

CHAPTER 36

Standing before the mirror in the change rooms, she inspected the red marks dotted about her neck. The advantage Ila had was painfully obvious. She was deadly when the fight went to the ground.

It occurred to Rose that if she had attacked Ila on the street, the girl could easily kill her!

Her eyes went wide at the strange realisation. Best not to dwell on it. The door swung open, and Ila swaggered in. Rose self-consciously grabbed a towel and threw it around her neck.

Ila gave her a friendly smile selecting a towel herself. "You good?" she asked. Rose just nodded. "I meant what I said, you've got some serious power behind those kicks."

"Doesn't mean much if I'm getting crushed on the ground," she said dejectedly. Tossing her towel aside, Ila guided a surprised Rose to the centre of the change rooms.

"When I come for your legs, like this…" She dropped to one knee and shot forward wrapping up Rose's legs. "…all you need to do is step away and press you weight down on my back," she said, demonstrating. "That's called a Sprawl. You basically just smother your opponent's attack."

Ila reset and went for the take down, Rose Sprawled on top of her, pushing her flat.

"Holy shit," she exclaimed. "That's easy!"

"Well, a good Jiu Jitsu practitioner will recover to the guard position."

"Huh?"

Ila quickly and fluidly adjusted her body, wrapped her legs around Rose's waist and dragged her down.

She was now trapped between Ila's legs.

"Oh…" Rose breathed in amazement.

The door flew open, and Cathy appeared. She opened her mouth to speak, but abruptly closed it when she saw the girls on the floor.

Rose on her knees, and Ila on her back with her legs wrapped around Rose.

"Shit, that was quick," Cathy said. "I usually make them buy me a drink first."

Rose stood quickly and awkwardly. Ila came to standing as graceful as a swan.

"Was just giving her some tips, coach," Ila said.

Cathy looked them up and down before speaking. "Well, you can give her whatever you want in your own time. Rose! Grab a mop, we got a bleeder out here." She sniffed and exited wordlessly.

The pair shared a sly look before bursting into laughter. "Sorry about her," Rose said. "She's a bit… you know…" She shrugged.

"It's all good, she's just old school. Michael says she was a gun back in her day. But there weren't any real fight comps for women back then."

"Well, thanks for showing me that stuff."

"No worries. I like sparring against you. You go pretty hard."

"That's something we have in common."

They shared a smile, before Ila snatched up her towel and headed toward the showers.

"Hey, I was just wondering," Rose called. "Where are you from exactly?"

Ila's smile dropped. She nodded to herself slightly, her face suddenly grim. Rose wondered if she'd just said something to piss off the girl who was capable of killing her.

"Australia," she said challengingly. Her body was suddenly tense, eyes hard.

Rose frowned, "Well yeah, obviously. I meant which suburb?"

The girl stared at her for a moment, then her body relaxed. "Oh, I thought you were asking about my...you know..." she gestured to her skin.

"No, I was wondering if you lived around here or..."

The girl rubbed her eyes with a laugh, "Sorry, I thought you meant something else...Flemington. I live near the flats in Flemington."

"No shit? My mum was from Flemington. I lived there when I was a kid!"

"Well, that's another thing we have in common," Ila said with a smile, and headed for the showers.

CHAPTER 37

The only light was the flickering of the television on the kitchen wall. She gently closed the front door and stole toward her room, desperate to avoid her mother. How the hell did Abdul sneak around so easily?

She was so close to her room now. If she could just slip in without her mother noticing, maybe she could talk with her properly in the morning.

"Ila?"

She sighed, dropping her bag before edging sheepishly into the kitchen. Her mother stood near the sink, arms folded, eyes unforgiving. "Where have you been?" Her tone indicated she already had the answer.

Ila made no reply. She knew what was coming.

"I'll ask you again," she said. Fixing her daughter in a glare of controlled rage. "Where have you been?"

"Training," she replied flatly. She could not raise her eyes to look at her mother. The glow of the television revealed the bruises and scratches from the afternoon's sparring session.

Her mother's anger faded. She looked on her daughter with dark, lost eyes. "I forbid you... but you do it anyway," she said, her voice tired and beaten.

Ila's natural want was to try to make her mother understand that *this* was her dream, and that it didn't mean she wouldn't strive for the other things her parents had fought to give her. She wasn't a child anymore. She understood that they had given everything to provide a safe life, and a path to a career that neither of them could ever have imagined for themselves.

She wanted to grab her mother and hug her, tell her all of those things. Instead, she remained silent. She knew her mother's mind was made up no matter what she said. So she chose to speak her truth. "I'm going to fight in the Warrior Challenge."

"Then you do not live here anymore."

"Rita, no!" They both swung to the pained voice. Her father stood in the hall. He looked as if he were struggling to hold himself upright. He wore his age more and more it seemed to her. "Rita, please. You are pushing her away," he said pleadingly.

"And now you care, Amir? You've been stuck in your own head for so long, that I have to play father as well!"

Ila couldn't bear to hear anymore. She picked up her bag, stalked passed her father and out into the night. Stepping out on to the street, she looked up at the thousand eyes of the flats. It felt as if they reflected her mother's eyes, cold and distant.

She hovered between worlds now. Not quite out into the world beyond, but no longer welcomed in the one where she had grown up. There was only one place left to her now, and it wasn't beneath the watchful eyes of the flats.

CHAPTER 38

Everyone gave Abdul and his boys plenty of room as they marched down the sidewalk. He felt the wary eyes of strangers on him as he passed, and an aloof grin slipped across his face. He could do whatever he wanted and not one of them would stop him. A stumble made him realise the booze was hitting him harder then he thought.

Throwing an arm around Marley's shoulders, he said, "We need more drinks, or maybe we hit the clubs?"

"Man, which club is going to let six wasted brothers in?" he laughed.

"They will if we get some girls," Abdul replied. "You know they let you in if you got some girls with you. Then they think you won't smash people."

Marly burst into laughter. "You're dreaming if you think any bitches want to hang with your ugly ass."

Abdul shoved his friend with a laugh. But then his fuzzy gaze landed on a group of girls waiting in line for one of the rooftop bars. One of the girls caught his eye and smiled coyly.

He nudged Marley, and the two shared a knowing grin. The whole group of girls were looking them over. Abdul sauntered toward them, and his boys followed. But as they headed toward them, a group of cops stepped on to the sidewalk from across the street.

Marley caught Abdul's arm. "You gotta be fucking shitting me!" he said pointing in disbelief at one of the cops.

The officer was older than them, maybe in his late twenties, and African.

"Fuck man, it's like seeing a white whale!" Marley cackled. The others joined in.

Except Abdul, who just stared as the police passed.

The opposing groups walked within a foot of each other but only Abdul and the African cop glared each other down.

Finally, the cop turned away, continuing on with his patrol. Abdul turned back to the girls. He didn't understand why, but he was sure he'd be seeing that white whale again.

CHAPTER 39

With no money for a taxi or ride share, and too late to catch the tram or train, Ila had walked the entire three suburbs distance to the gym.

She knew Michael would've shut the gym hours ago, and wanted it that way. She needed that quiet, that dark space again to think.

She didn't believe she could handle seeing him just now. Not because he'd done anything wrong. Ila just wanted to be alone.

As she turned the corner and saw the Atlas BJJ sign hanging over the doorway, the realisation that this could be the last night she would see her mother and father, hit her like a tonne of bricks.

Unlocking the door and slipping inside, she made sure that no one on the silent street had seen her enter.

Moving quickly into the darkness of the training area, she flopped exhausted on the mats. In the darkness of the gym she'd spent so much of the last seven years, she cried.

This was the only place that allowed her to be real.

She stayed on the mats until her tears dried. Then, wiping

the tears away, her eyes fixed on the punching bags lined against the far wall.

Illuminated softly by the yellow streetlights, they looked like dark canvases waiting to be coloured.

Retrieving her gloves from her bag, she rushed toward them unleashing a flurry of vicious strikes. There was no thought in her mind of technique or combinations. She struck hard, letting her emotion flow through her strikes. The tears were coming again. She let them fall with the force of her punches. Painting the blank canvas with her misery.

CHAPTER 40

It had been a brief, but exhilarating visit to the club. One of the girls had slipped Abdul a pill. They'd all hurried out into the night to one of the small parks near the Yarra River, which split through the city. It was only when they got there, that one of the boys had passed him and the others a bottle of vodka each.

"Where did you get these?" Marley drawled at their friend. He too was obviously high.

"Taxed them from that bar," their friend mumbled.

But Abdul was focused only on the girl on his lap, whose lips were locked on his, her tongue searching out his own. Her dark skin felt smooth and warm to the touch, and while he couldn't even remember her name, he was pretty sure she had no idea of his either. They kissed and fondled with a familiarity he hadn't felt with anyone before.

A part of him knew that was just the pill talking, but then the shattering of glass and the familiar words, "What the fuck are you looking at?" blunted his high instantly.

Breaking from his embrace, the girl spun to see what the commotion was all about. Untangling himself from her, he struggled to his feet.

As his vision cleared, he could see the boys fronting up to three other guys, but his vision was so blurred he couldn't really distinguish them. They were all just silhouettes against the flashing lights of the city.

"Aw man, not tonight!" he moaned as he made his way over.

Getting closer, he could see Marley getting in the face of one of these other guys.

He pushed his way between them, using his size to split the two factions apart. Only something was different. The three other guys weren't backing down.

Abdul felt a pang of anxiety as he took in the three men before him. They were solid, their faces grim, unflinching. These guys were used to fighting. He had a sense that they may have even been out looking for a rumble.

"Leave it, bro!" Abdul said, pushing his friend back. "We're having a good night, just let it go!"

"This guy wants smoke!" his friend spat drunkenly.

"I didn't say shit you little bitch," one of the men said calmly. "If you wanna go, then let's do it."

"Enough!" Abdul yelled. He shoved all his boys back hard. "Just fucken leave it, all right?"

He nodded to the girls huddled together away from the action. Clearly not sure if they should leave or stay. Luckily, the boys seemed to pick up on his meaning. Fight these three monsters and possibly get their heads caved in? Or go back to the girls and see where that led?

"Yeah well, next time then!" Marley yelled.

The men just laughed and turned to head on their way. Abdul sighed with relief. Crisis averted. He could go back to the warm embrace of his mystery woman.

"Typical black fucks," one of the men, said over his shoulder. "All fucking talk."

It was as if a switch was flicked in Abdul's mind. His hand clenched at his side. He spun around and walked up to the man who he was sure had spoken.

All he could think was hit and hit as hard as he could.

Throwing the punch with every ounce of rage and hate he had inside him, it landed sharply with the back of the man's head. He dropped instantly.

The sound of his head hitting the concrete was like an egg being cracked open.

Everyone just stopped and stared as blood pooled under the crumpled man's skull.

The other two howled in fury and threw themselves on Abdul. He didn't even really feel the hits despite their power, and even when he himself landed on the concrete, his eyes could not leave the vision of what he'd done. He'd been in dozens of fights and scraps, but he'd never heard a sound like that.

Nor seen someone lie so still after a punch.

In turn, his friends threw themselves at the two men. He caught a glimpse of the girls dashing away from the chaos.

Marley was there in his face all of sudden. "Abby! Bro, we gotta get out of here! Now!"

He was pulling him, trying to get him to move. But Abdul

could not take his eyes from the still body and pool of crimson.

Marley was suddenly gone. He heard his feet pounding on the pavement as he dashed from the park.

Someone crashed into him, flipping him over. Looking up in a daze, he found himself face to face with the cop he'd stared down earlier in the night.

Abdul thought the cop gave him an almost regretful sigh, as he pushed him on to his stomach, handcuffing him.

Other police were there now. The static voices from their radios and flash of approaching red and blue lights invaded the scene.

"Stay there, don't move," the cop grunted.

He was numb, as if this was all a dream he'd wake up from soon. But the sweet fantasy, the pill and the alcohol had weaved was faded now.

The harsh reality was written out before him in blood on the concrete.

CHAPTER 41

la lay in the deepness of sleep, dreaming nothing, thinking nothing. It was blissful silence.

A sudden flutter of light shook her from the sweet nothing. Sitting up groggily, she turned to approaching footsteps.

Michael was there, looking down on her, confusion written in his eyes. "What are you doing here?" he asked gently.

For a moment, she held him in her gaze, taking in this man that had been her coach, her friend and her confidante for the last seven years of her life.

They had grown together in a way, and now they were embarking on another stage of life. She couldn't do it without him, and she knew that he couldn't do it without her.

Hopping up suddenly, and taking his hand, she walked him out into the centre of the mats.

"What are you doing?" he demanded.

Sweeping his legs out from under him, she pressed her weight down. Still in confusion at what was happening Michael cried out in surprise. However, he instinctively defended and tried to sweep her off him.

He managed to gain the upper hand, but she swept him on

to his back again, using the technique he'd shown her all those weeks ago.

Now she was astride him. Both were breathing heavily. Neither made any attempt to move. He reached out a tentative hand around the back of her neck, and softly drew her to him.

He kissed her.

She returned it, and they fell into each other.

CHAPTER 42

The night was sticky and humid, and rather than trying to sleep, Rose had risen and gone for a run. The clock on her phone had told her it was three am when she had set off. She'd run so far that her legs had given up on her after a while. But she'd ignored the pain and run all the way back home.

One thought continued to chew at her.

Petra.

Still her friend wouldn't speak to her, wouldn't even respond to her texts. Rose used the frustration to fuel her on the way home.

It was just after six when she arrived out the front of home. Her legs were begging her to stop. Leaning against the front fence to catch her breath, she watched the rising sun. *No matter what happens, the sun always rises.*

A realisation struck her, and she pulled her phone from her pocket. Petra would be up by now. She had to get the early bus to make it to school on time.

Rose opened the message app and typed quickly before the urge left her. *'I'm sorry, please just let me talk to you.'*

She hit send. The panic returned, like an icy wind through her body.

If she didn't hear back from Petra this time, she knew she'd have to let her only real friend fade out of her life.

Her phone buzzed. A reply had landed! Holding her breath, she read.

'I can't.'

That was all? Frowning, she read it over and over.

'I can't.'

Rose squeezed her phone so hard, that she heard it crack in her grip. Stuffing it back in her pocket, she kicked open the back gate of the house. So, she was completely alone now? Well, that suited her just fine. She slammed the gate shut and entered the house. She'd been on her own most of her life anyway. This was nothing new. Within her the first flickers of rage were sparking.

Jo offered a welcoming smile as she entered, and Beth hurried from the table to hug her. The sight of the two was a reminder of why she was doing all this. She had to protect them. She attempted to douse the wildfire inside her. She refused to be like her dad and take out her problems on others.

"How was your run, love?" Jo asked.

"Good."

"You want some brekkie?"

Rose opened the fridge door. "Nah, I made some last night for us—" She stopped and stared, her anger flaring again. On the shelf in front of her were two empty plates.

"Sorry, love, I think your dad must have got into it when he got home last night."

Snatching one of the plates from the fridge she glared at it, her anger rising further. The bastard had not left one scrap on either plate.

Jo raised a hand to calm her. "Sorry, love. He had a big one last night, Collingwood got up in that final. You know how it is. I'll whip you up some eggs or something. Just let me get Beth ready," she said and began to fuss around on the stove.

But the flame wouldn't be doused, and in a fury she raised the plate above her head and smashed it on the ground with a shriek.

Beth recoiled from her in terror. Jo spun to the hallway. The fear in her eyes matching Beth's.

"What the fuck was that?" came a yell from her father's bedroom. Jo dropped to her knees and began gathering the shattered shards of the plate.

"He was sleeping it off," Jo stated, her eyes accusing.

They watched the entrance to the kitchen in fearful anticipation. Feet stamped down the hall toward them.

He stumbled in, looking more haggard than Rose had seen in a long time.

"Sorry, love," Jo said, her voice trying to give the tone of normality. "That was my fault, it must've just slipped out of my hands."

"Jesus Christ, Jo!" he pulled at his mess of hair, his eyes horribly blood shot. The stench of body odour and stale alcohol was so thick, Rose could taste it.

He looked from Jo to Beth, and then to her. She could see the rage in his face. And she wondered if he could see his own anger reflected.

He nodded darkly, taking them all in.

"I see. You're all testing me, aren't you?" he suddenly ripped Jo by the hair, tossing her roughly to the floor. She yelped in shock and pain. He kicked out viciously at her, as she lay huddled on the floor.

Beth ran to her mother and threw herself over Jo, tears streaming down her red cheeks.

He attempted to rip the child away, but Jo clutched her tight trying to shield her.

He kicked her again. But his kick went astray and struck Beth. The child screamed a horrific, pitiful sound.

That was it.

Rose lashed out, driven by her rage, and landed her front kick. He stumbled, crashing against the sink.

Jo and Beth went instantly silent.

They held each other and cowered as her dad pulled himself back to standing.

His red eyes looked demonic, as he turned them on her. "Have you lost your fucking mind?" he seethed.

Jo reached out to him. "Please don't hurt her—"

"Shut the fuck up!" he barked. He advanced on Rose. "You take a few classes and you think you can fuck with me in my own house?"

Rose breathed in and raised her fists.

He chuckled. "Don't raise your hands to *me* girl."

But she stood firm, heart racing, channelling the fear and the anger as he lunged toward her.

Rose delivered another horrific front kick to her father's stomach. He collapsed to his knees. As he grabbed the back of a chair to pull himself up, she unloaded her combinations on him.

Jab, right cross, left round house. He stumbled painfully, but she wasn't done.

Left upper cut, right hook, and then grabbing the back of his head, she wrestled her stunned father to the ground, and unloaded right hands on the side of his sweaty and greasy face.

The flame within was now an inferno. She roared, letting out the pain and rage. Letting out the years of fear.

A pair of tiny arms threw themselves around her neck. "Stop! Stop!" Beth pushed her way between Rose and her father.

"Stop, Rosie," she said in a small trembling voice as tears spilled down her puffy red face. "No more hitting! No more hitting!"

The rage fell away as she looked down on her sister's tiny trembling body. Then to the blood on her knuckles, and the blood dripping from her dad's nose and cheek.

A wash of panic struck, as the inferno guttered out. Beth was trembling in her arms now. Passing the child to Jo, she stood. Her own tears were falling. She looked down on the bloody mess of her dad's face. *So much red.*

"If you ever touch any of us again," she said, "I'll kill you."

Leaving the house was a blur, she was aware of Jo calling after her. But it wasn't until she came to the end of her street that she realised exactly what had happened.

Where could she go now?

Petra's was out of the question. The police? Well, not after what she'd just done.

It was a long walk, but she headed for the only other place that was open to her other than the streets.

Cathy's gym.

CHAPTER 43

She almost dropped with exhaustion when she arrived at the gym. The building and the street were quieter than usual. Her stomach grumbled. She hadn't eaten anything since yesterday, and her legs were quivering after all the running she'd done in the morning.

Her body felt ready to collapse when she pushed through the front door. Despite the warm morning sun cooking the street, the interior of the gym was icy and grim.

Rose called out into the gloom, hoping that Cathy was just late in opening. But when she heard a groan of a reply from the office, she slumped and moved toward the sound. She had a pretty clear idea of how her coach had spent her night.

Barging in without waiting to be invited, she found Cathy reclining in her chair, feet on the desk.

It was clear she hadn't slept, and probably had forgotten to even lock the front door last night.

She looks worse than dad. An empty bottle of white wine lay on the desk and, as always, a bottle of vodka was in her hand.

"Hey! Look who the fuck it is!" Cathy blurted, before slumping forward on to the desk.

"You're pissed," Rose accused.

"Literally and figuratively," Cathy slurred back. Rose was genuinely amazed she was able to form the words.

"Ange dropped by with his fucking goons last night," she continued. "Took the last of me bloody money. I'm done. I can't do this shit anymore..." She trailed off and took a swig of vodka.

Rose felt the anger rising again, her face growing hot. But she took a breath, doing her best to calm herself. "You said you'd train me," she stated, folding her arms like a disappointed parent.

Cathy shook her head. "I'm shutting it down. Were done," she said with a dismissive wave.

"Why?" Rose demanded.

Forcing herself to standing, Cathy stumbled to a filing cabinet as she slurred, "Because, I can't afford to keep this place open anymore. Ange has finally fucked me! Here, see this?" She brandished a sheet of paper at Rose. "I sign this, and your community service bullshit is done."

She picked up a pen from the desk, scribbled on the bottom of the page and threw it at Rose. "Now fuck off home." She tried to collapse back into her chair but missed it and plunged to the floor with a thud. She lay still, eyes struggling to open.

A weary despondency fell upon Rose.

She reached for the paper but paused with her hand outstretched. If she took it, she could simply walk away. She'd be free from the law, and maybe it would be good to completely wipe her slate clean. That was unless her dad called the cops.

But given his distaste for the boys in blue, that seemed unlikely.

Instead, she left the paper where it lay, and grabbing Cathy's thick ankles, dragged the woman from the office.

Cathy yelled something, but her words were little more than incoherent grunts and moans.

Rose wasn't going to give up on this woman, even if she'd given up on herself.

Kicking open the change room door, she headed for the showers.

Cathy had faded into her drunken slumber, as if the act of being dragged across the floor was somehow like being rocked to sleep.

Rose dumped her coach unceremoniously in the shower cubical, wrenched the cold-water tap to blast, and stepped back.

For a moment Cathy was still as ice-cold water pounded her. But then her eyes shot open. Cursing and thrashing around in the shower cubical, she tried to get her footing. The coach was soaked in an instant.

Somehow the red bandana stayed on her head.

Cathy gained her footing, and barrelled toward Rose, grabbing her by the scruff of the neck and slamming her against the wall.

"You little fucker!" she yelled.

Rose grabbed at the elder woman and yelled back, "You're just the same as everyone else! You don't give a fuck about anyone but yourself!"

"I've done this longer than you've been alive, you little shit!"

"And now you're just giving up?"

"You think I haven't tried everything to keep this place going? How do you think I got in with Angelo in the first place?" Now tears welled in her eyes, but still her grip was firm. "This place is all I have," she hissed, her words suddenly free from the drunken slurring. "This is all I am."

Releasing Rose, she slid down the opposite wall. The shower still spewed the icy water, and it filled the air, causing Cathy's warm breath to mist as she spoke. "I took a lot of money from Ange to keep this place going; to try and live up to dad's reputation." She shrugged hopelessly. "But Ange is a shark, he's got me by the balls, and he knows it. I can't pay him back. I'd hoped to get more people through the doors but with the businesses in the area closed. Well… not many people out this way now."

"But, if you get him the money, he goes away, right?"

She laughed up at Rose. "Kid, pricks like him never really go away."

Rose had an idea though. She knew it was ridiculous, she knew Cathy would laugh even harder, but after what she'd been through this morning, what did she have to lose?

"What about this?" she said as she whipped out her phone and typed into the search engine. Rose held it out to Cathy who squinted drunkenly at the screen.

Cathy scoffed. "That stupid Warrior comp?"

"We could enter."

"We?"

"I can fight!" Rose insisted.

But Cathy laughed again, slapping her hand in the growing puddles of water. "You've done one sparring session!"

"So? I'll do more. None of the other guys you train are entering."

"That's because they know they'll get smashed! You think you're fucking Rocky or something? That is a Mixed Martial Arts tournament. People get hurt doing this shit. Hurt badly!"

"Yeah? Well, I'm used to it!"

The coach rubbed her heavy eyes, and struggled to her feet. Shutting off the shower, she rounded on her slowly. "Why do you care if I have to shut down or not? You've only been here a few weeks—"

"Because this is all I have now! I have nothing else left! Nothing!"

They looked each other over, and Rose saw a thousand thoughts running through Cathy's head.

Was this the right thing to do? Go in for a competition where trained fighters, amateurs or not, tried to beat you into unconsciousness in the hope that she could win some money to keep a deadbeat gym going?

Rose thought back to her session against Ila. Could she really stand toe-to-toe against girls like that in the long run? But there was more to it than just trying to keep the gym going. Rose felt a path of sorts being laid out before her. She prayed Cathy could see it too.

"We have a lot of work to do before then," Cathy grumbled.

"Starting with emptying the bins?" Rose grinned.

"No, starting with getting me a bloody towel!"

CHAPTER 44

S itting on unforgiving plastic seats, they waited in silence for the return of Abdul's lawyer. Ila tapped her foot nervously as they waited.

Despite surviving, the injuries that Abdul's victim had suffered were severe. There had been a lot of media hype around the case, and as a result, her brother's initial hearing was a closed court.

Her mother stared blankly at the floor. Ila wondered what she was thinking. Was she blaming herself for Abdul's actions? Or was she simply trying to mentally distance herself from the whole situation. She'd barely spoken a word since the call from the police had come.

Abdul's lawyer came down the hallway and stopped in front of them. "Bail has been refused," he reported. "The prosecution is pushing to have him charged under the 'Coward Punch legislation'. He's looking at a mandatory sentence."

Seeing that her mother wasn't acknowledging him, he frowned then addressed Ila. "You're the sister?"

She nodded.

He continued. "I'm afraid with all the other charges, plus

the fact that he was supposed to be on a community service, which he didn't attend once, it's not looking good. He'll be held in custody until his next appearance."

She rubbed her eyes and nodded defeated.

"I've been able to get you some time with him, but we better hurry."

He turned and strolled away. She stood and followed, but realised her mother was still sitting.

"Mum?"

But she continued to stare down at the floor.

"Miss?" the lawyer called. "We really must hurry."

Ila turned away from her mother and followed.

*

A guard led her to a holding room, ushered her inside and lent against the door.

Abdul sat on a bench against the wall. His eyes lit up when she entered. But then the light was replaced with a clear and heavy shame, and he cast his eyes to the floor.

"Two minutes," the guard announced gruffly, as she moved over to her brother.

He couldn't look at her now, nor was she certain of exactly what to say. What words would help? Should she tell him not to worry? That it would all be all right in the end. Or should she yell and scream at him? Why had he done it? Did he have brains in his head, or had he smoked them all to mush?

She wanted to yell, to scream, to cry.

Instead, she slid an arm around him. He dropped his head into her shoulder.

They stayed there in silence, until the guard tapped his watch, and led her from the room.

As she wandered back down the hall, she heard her brother's sobs.

Her tears followed.

*

Without a word, her mother left the courthouse. However, Ila reflected that she had not exactly pushed the conversation either. So, after some consideration, she decided to walk the long distance back to their house and offer the olive branch of peace.

It was late afternoon when she unlocked the door and entered quietly. There was no sign of her mother's car outside, was anyone home at all? Then two pairs of little feet came pounding toward her down the hall. Squatting, Ila spread her arms wide to embrace Evie and Mohammed. They crashed into her arms, and bombarded her with questions. Where had she been? What was she doing? Was it true she was going to be a fighter? Would she be staying home now?

She didn't answer. How could she when she had no idea of the answers herself? Holding her little siblings to her, feeling the beating of their excited hearts and basking in their innocent smiles, she felt more tears rising but she sniffed them back; she would be strong for them.

"Ila? Is that you?" her father's strained voice called from her parent's bedroom.

She ushered the twins into the living room where the television was blaring away then headed up the hallway to her parents' room. Ila cautiously opened the door. Her father smiled up at her, but his sullen eyes told her a different story. He was struggling with something within, that much was clear.

But then she saw what he cradled. Her purple Jiu Jitsu belt.

He patted the bed next him, and she sat. His eyes went down to the belt. "Do only girls wear purple?" he asked in his broken accent.

She shook her head kindly. "No. They use the belts to signify your level of ability and experience. It's sort of like my rank."

He nodded his understanding. "Purple is a high rank?"

"Sort of. Still a lot to learn though."

He indicated the white tips on the end of the belt. "And these?"

"When you earn four of these, then you're almost ready to go to the next belt."

"Ah! Earning your stripes!" he said proudly. "I have heard of this."

She giggled at his excitement and understanding. But then his face dropped again. "You must've worked hard for this," he said.

She nodded. "It's my dream to do it as my job, you know… maybe one day."

Folding the belt in his lap, his gaze became distant. It was like he was allowing his mind to wonder deeper than he usually did.

"Dad? You ok?"

He took her hand. "I made a dream too when I was your

age. I dreamed of somewhere safe, and I promised I would fight to make it to that place. I thought, 'If I am blessed to have a family, they will never need to fight at all, because I will do it for them.'" He squeezed her hand, and for a second, she thought she saw the beginning of tears forming in his eyes. But he held her with his gaze, and spoke on.

His voice even, but soft. "We were trying to escape from the killing," he continued. "But we were captured not far from the border. The general of the militia said to us, we could fight for him, or we could die in the morning. But we knew that either way he was going to kill us. Because they think we are rebels."

She held her hand up. "Dad, you don't have to tell me this—"

"No. I must," he said simply. "When they dropped their guard, we ran again. Nothing can make a man run like the fear of losing his life. When we were two days from the border, my friend, Omari, lay down to sleep. We couldn't get him up again." A tear escaped her father's eye. "He was first to die."

Taking a breath, he wiped the tear from his cheek and continued. Ila gripped his hand in hers, realising how bad her own hands were shaking.

"Nasif, my other friend, tried to find help. He walked north into the bush. We never saw him again. My cousin Rashad had directed us the whole way. But when the general's men caught up to us... he… he just couldn't run any more. He led them off, so I could escape. He said to me, 'I hope one day we can come home?' Maybe one day, I said."

He was reliving the journey right in front of her, and she wanted so badly to hug him, to stop him torturing himself. But she knew this was a story he needed to finish, and that maybe the story finished with her.

"I alone made it to the border," he said. "I met your mother there, in the refugee camp. She had fire in her then too. She would not let me give up. My body escaped, my mind did not. But always, I held on to my dream."

He placed the belt in her quivering hands. "If this is your dream, then you must fight for it."

She embraced him.

In the other room, the sound of the twins' laughter drifted to her, and she felt the realisation that he had found his dream, and gifted it to his children.

CHAPTER 45

Rose clutched the toilet bowl and vomited again. Her whole body shook with nerves. Cold sweat ran down her face. It had only been a week since they'd decided to go for the Warrior tournament, and despite the fact she had lived and breathed nothing but training, the reality off her first proper fight was terrifying.

This was the only opportunity she'd get before the tournament.

She had to make the most of it.

A banging on the cubical door made her jump. "Oi! You good in there?" Cathy's rough voice boomed.

"Y-yeah!" she stammered back.

"Well hurry, we've only got a couple of minutes before we're on." She heard the toilet door crash open as Cathy left.

Rose flushed her spew and stepped out of the cubical. After washing her face, she straightened and eyed herself in the mirror. The fight gear they'd ordered still hadn't arrived, so Rose had borrowed a pair of MMA shorts, ankle guards and a singlet that was one annoying size too big, and hung just off her shoulder.

Cathy had platted her hair back in cornrows, and it had been sort of weird for her to see her own face completely uncovered. She never realised that she'd used the veil of her hair to hide behind.

So here she was, her first amateur fight. All entrance to the Warrior competition must have at least one amateur win under their belt.

Cathy had to pull a few strings with some of her connections to get this fight, and they'd even had to turn a slightly blind eye to the fact that Rose's registration as a fighter was still processing. Not to mention the weight difference between her and the opponent. Although, they hadn't told her who her opponent was, or who was bigger. Cathy assured her, it wouldn't be easy but it would be fair.

So here she was...

"Come on," she urged herself. "This should be a breeze compared to dealing with Dad." She giggled, somewhat manically and walked out into the change room area.

It was time.

*

The community hall the fights were being held in was surprisingly full. Cathy had said this was the last round of amateur fights before the Warrior competition.

"Don't think about the audience," Cathy said, as they waited by the cage. "Most are just waiting to see their friend or brother, or who the fuck ever fight. They don't care about you, so don't care about them."

Cathy's advice helped slow the frantic beating of her heart, but as the official strapped on her gloves and checked her over, Rose looked out on all the faces in the crowd and her stomach lurched again.

Cathy directed her into the cage, and then went to her spot on the outside. Rose had to grip the cage's wire to stay upright, her head was spinning so much.

What the fuck am I doing in here? Why did I think this was a good idea?

"You right?" Cathy asked through the wire.

Rose was surprised by the tone of genuine concern. She nodded finally managing to contain her emotions. After all, how was this really any different then sparring in the gym?

She realized Cathy was still talking to her and tuned in. "You'll be fine. Just keep your distance, and throw your combinations off the leading strike, got it?"

She nodded.

"Your opponent has a Thai Kickboxing background, so she probably won't try to grapple with you."

"Where the hell is she?" Rose asked. Cathy nodded to the entrance of the cage.

Rose's fear instantly struck back with vengeance when she beheld the woman she'd have to go through just to enter the Warrior Competition. The fighter had to be in her late twenties. Her arms were coated in tattoos, and her platinum hair was tied back in such a way, that it gave her the appearance of some kind of Viking barbarian.

She belongs on some forgotten battleground, wielding an axe. Not in modern society!

She spun to Cathy, making no attempt to hide her terror.

"Don't give me that look," Cathy said, "This was *your* idea." But then she softened and drew Rose in. "Listen, range and distance. Remember, it's her first fight too. She's probably just as scared as you."

Rose only needed to glance at the Viking's cruel smile to know that certainly was not the case.

The referee called them to the center of the cage, pulling them in close, "Ok ladies, obey my instructions at all times, nothing to the back of the head and watch the low shots. Touch gloves now and come out fighting."

Rose held out her fists to touch gloves, but the Viking just stared back at her. A smug grin was all she offered.

"Do it!" the referee ordered, but the Viking just backed away, that smug confidence oozing from every pore.

Can't be any worse than Dad, Rose reminded herself.

Then suddenly the bell sounded, and she didn't have time to worry about being afraid.

Moving lightly on her feet toward the Viking, she used her jab and front kick to find her range. She was stunned to land thumping strikes on the woman. Her confidence grew, and she unleashed a savage kick to the inside of her opponent's front leg, hissing with satisfaction as the kick landed. She expected to see the Viking crumple.

However, to her horror, the woman smiled her smug grin and advanced. She had simply been sizing her up this whole time.

The Viking dispatched a jab like a whip. Rose saw a flash

of white as she was struck and staggered. It was followed up by a stinging roundhouse kick to her thigh, which caused her to crumble to the ground with a yelp. An audible wince hissed from the watching crowd.

Rose covered up, bracing for the ground assault. But the Viking stepped back and waved her to standing.

"Hands up and move!" Cathy yelled.

Struggling up, she hobbled around the cage, much to the amusement of this monster.

For the remainder of the round the Viking delivered smooth, and crippling shots to Rose's body. She seemed to be able to strike in just the right place to cause maximum pain. The woman's shins were like iron rods, and her fists felt like anvils in wrapped gloves. But Rose refused to stop retaliating, much to the growing amusement of the Viking, whose smile slowly turned to a hateful sneer. Mercifully, the bell sounded for the end of the round, and the referee pushed them apart.

He followed Rose as she staggered back to her corner. "You keep getting hit like that, and I have to stop the fight, understand?"

"Yeah, we understand, knucklehead!" Cathy yelled at him. She began to towel the sweat from Rose's brow. "Don't worry, kid, you've got her in two minds, she doesn't know whether to hit you in the body or the head!"

Rose shot her an unimpressed scowl.

Cathy held up a hand in apology. "Not the right time to joke, fair point."

"What the fuck am I doing out here?" Rose despaired.

"Listen," Cathy said, grabbing her face in her hands. "So, she's a bit of a psycho and a bloody good striker. But she's overconfident now, and even though she throws them like a tornado, she's overreaching and dropping her hands."

"But what the fuck *do I do*?"

"Listen! Whenever she throws anything, it's coming straight down the line. Sit back, wait for her to throw, parry the strike and counter with the right roundhouse. Just sit back and wait. Let her come at you!"

"That's all? Just wait for her to come at me?"

Cathy nodded as the ten second warning was called. "Just keep it simple!"

She grabbed her ice bucket and towel to leave, but then whipped back to Rose. "And keep your hands up!"

The bell sounded. The Viking eased herself from her stool, stretching lazily. Her trainer hurried out of the cage, and it was locked behind him.

Rose did her best not to succumb to the frustrated rage simmering inside her. It wouldn't be much help against this behemoth. Nor would descending back into fear be any use. She'd survived the first round, although she was pretty sure that was only because the Viking had let her.

Now she had to implement this supposed game plan Cathy had given her.

Rose moved waiting for the first strike to come.

If she could land a few shots, maybe she could build up her points.

But the Viking whipped out her right hand, like it had been

shot from a rocket launcher. Had the punch landed, Rose would have been crushed under the power of the strike. However, on pure reaction she parried the blow with her left hand, then she fired her right round house high at the Viking's head.

Her shin cracked against the woman's temple. She staggered, looked at Rose as if she was seeing her for the first time, then tumbled to her knees heavily.

Everyone, the ref, the audience, the judges and officials let out a gasp of shock. They stared, not really comprehending what had just happened. Even Rose just gawked in amazement.

"Now!" Cathy screamed, leaping up and down on the spot. "Get on her!"

Rose snapped back to the moment and dived on the Viking. Gaining the strong mount position quickly, she threw down punch after punch.

The woman covered up but was too dazed to mount any kind of real offence, or even defend properly.

When her hands fell limply away, Rose pounded three consecutive right hands to the side of the woman's head.

The apathetic crowd erupted at the quick change in fortunes. The referee dived in and waved the fight off. "Stop! She's done!" he yelled. Rose fell back against the cage, her hands to her face in bewilderment.

Cathy clambered over the cage, embracing her in a bear hug.

"I won?" Rose asked, still not really understanding what had just happened.

"Where the fuck did that even come from?" Cathy screamed

as she bounced up and down on the spot.

"I... I just did what you said." Rose couldn't believe she'd just knocked out the Viking.

"And best of all..." Cathy cupped her hands around Rose's face. "You kept your bloody hands up!"

*

A silence now hung over the change rooms, like a storm had just passed. Rose and Cathy had stayed to watch the remainder of the fights on the card, and she'd been amazed at the variety of combative skills on show.

She noted that there were simple patterns that she was able to predict. If a fighter was a grappler, or Jiu Jitsu practitioner, they tried to take the fight to the ground as quickly as possible. If the fighter came from a striking discipline, such as kickboxing or Mauy Thai, they tried to keep the fight standing. Then there were some fighters that looked comfortable both fighting standing or wrestling on the ground. Those were the ones she was concerned about. They were just as happy to be lying on their backs fighting, as they were to be standing toe to toe.

She was snapped from her thoughts as a little girl, roughly the same age as Beth, ran from the entrance door of the change rooms, through to the shower area.

Leaning back from packing her bag, she looked to see where the hell this kid was going. The child ran toward a figure hunched over on the bench in front of the running shower.

"Mummy!" the little girl cried launching into the woman's arms. "Are you ok?"

The woman scooped her up, and Rose could see who it was.

"I am now," said the Viking, wrapping her daughter in a loving embrace.

Rose finished packing and slipped quietly from the room.

CHAPTER 46

C athy placed Rose's trophy on the shelf above the office door. It was late now, and the adrenaline from the fight had faded. Rose felt totally numb, even the bruises, and the cuts from the fight, didn't really hurt. It was a strange, emotionless feeling, and one that was a little disconcerting. She'd never felt anything like this.

"You all right?" Cathy asked in that disinterested tone of hers.

Rose nodded and gazed up at the gold trophy.

"We've qualified as the only wild card entrance into the Warrior comp. But we've got one problem. There are no more amateur fights between then and now."

Rose nodded, her eyes fixed on the trophy. "I've never won anything before," she said, as if sensing Cathy's next question.

But the coach gave a sigh, then physically turned Rose to look at her. "It's just a step, not the end. You have a chance to turn your life around. That's really the only reason I'm doing this," she said, gesturing to the pair of them. "You can use this whole experience to change things for yourself. That should be your goal, not a piece of plastic painted gold." Cathy slapped her on the shoulder.

Rose nodded her thanks as Cathy headed into the office. She understood the coach's words, but still, she couldn't take her eyes off her prize.

*

She chanced sleeping at home that night, but snuck in late, and was out early. Rose was pretty sure her dad was out on a bender. Collingwood had lost their Saturday night preliminary final thus ending their season. So he would have either come home smashed and fallen asleep – hopefully not touching Jo – or he would've stayed out with his dead shit mates all night, and crashed on one of their couches.

Either way, she didn't see him and that was just fine with her. Rose walked the long distance toward the gym, only to realise it was way too early for it to be open, so she headed to the local shopping center and strolled around, taking mental stock of her many sore joints and bruises as she pondered what could be on the cards for training today.

Stepping around a corner, she stopped with a jolt. Before her was a girl browsing the window of some high-end store, a bag of groceries in her hand. Her hair was platinum blonde, and Rose felt a stab of panic as the girl turned in her direction.

Tierney stumbled back when she realised who was standing before her. Her once beautiful, tanned face was a mess of fading stitches and scars. Her left eye still bloodshot and partly closed, there was a horrible purple shade beneath it. Tierney stared at Rose like she'd just walked into the Grim Reaper himself.

Rose's panic turned to guilt, as she beheld the horrific

extent of what she'd done to the queen. Being no medical expert, she still knew that those scars would never fully heal. She'd marked Tierney for life.

Rose opened her mouth to speak, although what she would say, she had no idea. But before she could attempt to say anything, Tierney turned and bolted.

Rose toyed with the idea of trying to catch up to her and... and... well, she really had no idea what she'd say. She'd never wanted to hurt someone that badly.

I could have killed her.

A swirl of regret and desperation to make things right filled her. But what could she do? Nothing would make it better. No number of apologies would ever make it better.

Her father drifted into her thoughts now, and she pictured how badly she beaten him. He, of all people, deserved it. But had it solved anything? If she could do that to a grown man, and could hurt a girl so bad that she would bear the marks of the beating for the rest of her life, maybe she needed to gain a new understanding of what violence was. Where anger could really lead.

The rage that came to her was dangerous. She understood that now. And to mix the rage with these new skills she was learning could be horribly lethal. This lesson was learned the hard way, and it had taken someone else's suffering for her to understand it.

She swore to herself she wouldn't fight outside the cage or the ring again. If she were truly going to set herself on this new path, as Cathy had said, she would have to embrace a different approach to her life.

And one big problem she had was at home, with Jo and Beth. Rose slung her bag over her shoulder and turned back toward home.

CHAPTER 47

C athy rubbed the bridge of her nose, but it did little to stop the flood of pain through her head. After the excitement of their win yesterday, she'd expected to be bouncing into the next day with energy and enthusiasm, but her energy was sapped, and her body shuddered every few minutes, as if she were fighting off a flu.

She was used to feeling a bit dusty in the morning, but that was understandable when she'd sunk half a bottle of vodka the night before.

But this was different.

She hadn't drunk at all last night. The thrill of the win had been a big enough buzz for her. It dawned on her that the reason she was feeling like she'd just gone ten rounds with a vodka bottle was because she was having a withdrawal from *not* drinking. This was good, wasn't it? Sure, her head ached like hell, but at least she wasn't holding in vomit while training a fighter.

Maybe when she'd spoken to the kid about putting herself on a new path, she'd been convincing herself as well. The thought of having a drink hadn't even occurred to her today.

She grinned at the photo of her dad sitting on the desk. *I'm making progress, Dad!*

The clang of the front door opening dragged her from her thoughts, and she headed out.

The three men standing before her sent her into a whip of fearful panic, yet she refused to show it. Cathy wouldn't give them the satisfaction of thinking they could frighten her.

"Bomber!" Angelo called in mock excitement.

His two goons flanked him, arms folded.

"How are we today girl?"

She ignored him, and simply opened the cash draw, scooped out the notes and held them out.

He gave a triumphant grin, motioning for one of his men to collect. The man snatched the money from her. Counted it, and shook his head with a dismissive scoff.

"And the rest of my cash?"

Without intending to, her eyes flickered to the poster on the wall for the Warrior Heart competition. He didn't miss the look of desperation, and her glance at the poster.

"What? You putting one of your fighters in that?" He laughed. "Shit, Bomber, things must be getting pretty desperate if that's your answer."

Her eyes dropped, she knew it was a stupid idea, and in fairness she'd been drunk when she'd agreed to it. But the kid was giving it everything and despite the fact the kid wouldn't win, what did they really have to lose? *Well, the gym for one thing.* But she pushed that worry away.

Perhaps she'd get a chance to wipe that smug look off

Angelo's face. His expression changed to a dour one, and with it the whole energy in the room seemed to shift. The two thugs on either side were itching to have another shot at her.

She could feel it.

But instead, he spoke low and direct, his finger in her face. "Don't fuck me over, Bomber. I've had enough of this crap, and you've had more than enough opportunity. I will get what's owed me, one way or another." He straightened and looked to the poster with a sly grin. "Best of luck with the fights, champ!"

They swaggered out. Only when she heard the sound of their car drive away, did she breathe again.

Powering back into the office, she headed straight for the bottle of vodka in her desk. But stopped as she reached a trembling hand for it.

No.

I have to be on top of this. The kid is counting on me. She took the bottle and tipped the sour smelling liquor down the drain in the kitchenette.

She wasn't going to give up everything her father had left her, and everything he had taught her to stand for, without a fight.

She owed him, the kid, and herself that much at least.

CHAPTER 48

Rose had been ducking her father since their fight, but knew eventually they'd have to face up again. Now was the time. If she was going to embrace this new path, then her dad was one obstacle she just couldn't avoid any longer.

What was going to happen this time? Would she be able to talk to him? Neither of them talked much to the other, even in better circumstances.

Their street was looking very pleasant in its sundrenched state. The balmy weather seemed a paradox to the confrontation that was about to happen. Now she was here, she didn't really know exactly what to do.

Just barge in?

Maybe call the pigs first? She thought about calling David, her caseworker, but he would just contact the pigs anyway.

She threw out a prayer to whichever God might be listening and stepped to the door. Unlocking the screen and then the front door, she slipped inside.

The air thick and musty, and barely a ray of light found its way through the curtains. As her eyes adjusted to the dark, the sound of sobbing came to her. A lamp was flicked on, illuminating the room in a dirty yellow glow.

Jo huddled against the armrest of the couch. Her hair was a mess, and her eyes bruised and bloodshot.

Rose's hands clenched at her sides, but Jo shook her head. Then the familiar slurred voice of her father dribbled from the shadows.

"Hey look! Fucking Wonder Woman is back," he drooled.

He was sitting on the other end of the couch. Beth perched on his lap, her cheeks streaked with tears.

Her hands clenched tighter at her sides. She would rip him to shreds if he'd done anything to Beth.

"Beth… are you ok?" she whispered in as gentle a voice she could muster, trying to give the child a beguiling smile. Beth said nothing but reached her arms toward her sister.

"Don't talk to her," he mumbled as he sipped a can of Woodstock. "We've been waiting all morning for you, ever since I got home." He lent forward and she could smell the familiar, rich stench of alcohol. "You and me got some things to discuss," he growled. "You've tested me, Rosie, and now I'm going to test you."

Beth's tears flowed and she stretched out desperately to Jo. "Shh…" he cooed. "It's all right, Daddy isn't going to let her hurt you or anyone else, ever again."

The rage was welling up, ready to explode. But he'd been smart, or maybe ruthless was a better word? He'd put the last two people she had between them. He was using her love for them as a shield.

"If you've fucking touched either of them—"

"You know, I remembered something very interesting this morning," he interrupted. "If you get arrested again, you go straight into custody. So, imagine if I call the cops, and tell them about the assault you did to me, your own father no less."

He sneered up at her. Beth began wailing as she hung forward, desperate and terrified. Slipping from her father's rough grip around her neck, until he tightened his hold.

"Let her go!" Rose ordered.

But he ignored her still. "So, I got an idea on how we can make this all even," he announced. "Rosie, I want you to go to my room and get my belt from the back of the door and bring it here. Because I am going to whip the fucking skin off you—"

"Nathan! Enough!" Jo screeched. She was near hysterical, and reaching for Beth.

"Shut up," he screamed back.

Beth's crying was now the droning soundscape behind them. He slumped back, Beth still hanging with his hand around her neck. She had the image of a hunting dog holding some poor bird in its jaws.

Stepping toward this thing that was ruling over their lives, her rage began bubbling like a boiling kettle. If she could smash that Viking woman, she could smash him, and besides she'd done it before—

No.

Uncurling her fists, she cooled the flame of rage. This was not the way. She had to try something else, and she had an idea what.

"Can I ask you something?" she said calmly. Her father

smiled, and took another sip from his Woodstock can. "What kind of man wants to fuck his own daughter?"

He spat the drink out and lurched to his feet. Beth tumbled to the floor with a thud. Jo swooped in taking the child into her arms. Rose backed up toward the front door. She slipped her key from her pocket, keeping a wary eye on her swaying father.

His face went red with rage. "You little shit," he screamed. "You want to try me again? You were lucky, you hear me? Lucky!"

He lurched toward her, but she slipped out of the door. Grabbing the screen door, she slammed it shut. By the time he made it to her, she had locked it. He wrapped on it over and over.

"Jo!" he called. "Get my fucking key! Now!"

Rose whipped out her phone, dialing quickly.

"Who are you calling? Unlock the bloody door!"

"Police," Rose said to the emergency operator.

Her father's face dropped instantly at the word. He tried again to push the screen door open, but while it bent and groaned the lock held.

"Four Seven Two, Westgarth Terrace, North River," she said, eyeing her father.

"An assault."

"Rosie," he begged.

"My dad, Nathan Tanner."

"Open the fucking door!"

She held the phone up as he yelled and kicked at the door. He went silent. But it was too late. She could tell from the glazed stare of fear, that he knew the operator would have heard him clear as day.

"Please hurry!" Rose said, giving a fake, dramatic sob. "He's already bashed my step-mum."

He was still. The same look she'd seen on Jo's face every time he entered a room drunk or came home from watching his football team lose, was plastered on his face.

The operator assured her the police were only minutes away. She hung up.

"Don't test me," she hissed unlocking the screen door and pushing past him. She sat on the couch and embraced Beth and Jo. He looked to the street, then back at them.

She could tell he had no idea where to go or what to do. He turned and stumbled down the hall to his bedroom.

A weight slipped from her mind. Together the three women sat. Rose thought of the plastic trophy sitting above Cathy's office door. Her coach had been right. There were more important things to fight for then a piece of plastic painted gold.

CHAPTER 49

Ila woke on the morning of the fight, in a warm bed next to the man she loved, and asked herself, 'why?'.

Why was she doing this? Going to a competition where she would have to possibly fight three different opponents to win overall. What on Earth possessed her to want to do this?

Ila thought how nice it would be to play the safe game. To explain to Michael that her family needed her now that Abdul was gone. While she was sorry to let him down, she hoped that he would understand.

Why not simply focus on her studies, train occasionally with Michael, and maybe she could just run a few classes for him. They could build a life together. It could be an enjoyable and comfortable life, doing what they loved, and doing it together. No more punches to the face, or arguments with her mother.

All this raced through her mind as she slipped out of bed, and prepared for fight day.

Why was she doing this?

She did it for her father, who had fought to give her the opportunity to follow her dreams. She was doing it for her mother, who despite her iron-clad strictness, had shown her what was possible if you truly dedicated yourself to it.

She did it for her younger siblings, to set them a strong example of hard work and commitment.

She did it for Abby, to show him there was another path. A path that could lead to a positive life, that could lift you from the flat trajectory you were on.

She did it for Michael, who had been beside her from day one when she walked into his gym and asked if she could try this weird thing called Jiu Jitsu.

Above all else, she did it for herself.

This was the one thing in her life that truly empowered her. That both humbled her, and yet strengthened her.

It was her dream to be a professional fighter.

That was why.

*

Even Michael was taken back by the size of the crowd packed into the community hall. Ila thought she spotted some nerves in him as he signed them in and spoke with officials.

Banners from other gyms hung around the hall, and it seemed each gym had a rather large contingent of supporters scattered throughout the venue.

The previous day had been the men's competition, which had turned out to be a roaring success. "Everyone loves watching a tear up!" Michael joked.

The afternoon moved quickly. Every time she cast a glance to the clock, the hands had jumped forward.

Mingling with the crowd, they listened to the announcer

in the cage before the competition officially kicked off. He informed them all that each match would hold three, three-minute rounds. The tournament was a knock-out competition, meaning simply that if you lost, you were out.

The only way to win the ten grand, and the tournament, was to be the last one standing.

Ila's game plan hadn't changed. She would attempt to bring every fight to the ground. That was where she could dominate. But as she looked around the change room at the other women warming up, she noticed quite a few were practicing their wrestling and ground-work.

Moving with strength, grace and an eerie calm, these women were not here just to have some fun. They were here to win.

"Nervous?" Michael ventured as he wrapped her hands. She was changed, warmed up, and as ready as she could be. She nodded, watching him as he worked.

"Yeah, me too," he admitted gently. They shared a forced smile. He finished wrapping her hands and took hold of them, "Two fights, that's all it is. You win them and you're through to the final!" he slapped her leg encouragingly. "Ten grand, Ila! Easy money!"

Glancing at her nearest opponent, who unloaded brutal roundhouse kicks on the pads her trainer held, she had a feeling this day would be many things, but certainly not easy.

He took her hand again. "Everything you've done on the mats in the gym, all the sparring over the last seven years has led up to this moment," he said. "Sure, these girls are all beasts, but you're the lion!" he jabbed a finger into her chest.

A smirk broke across her lips. "Great rev up, coach."

He slumped, "I've been working on it all week actually."

"I can tell," she said. "It was very well rehearsed."

"Listen, will you just go out there, and choke some bitches?"

"That I can do," she said with a smile.

An official stuck his head in the room and bellowed, "Show time, ladies! First fight Abara and Valdez. Fighters to the cage!"

Michael helped her to her feet, doing a quick final check of his equipment as he did.

She realised who the girl throwing the savage kicks on the pads was.

Rose! The kid from the gym on the North Side! Her mouth dropped open at the recognition. She was fighting today? Her mouth dropped wider when she saw just how hard the kicks were landing.

Cathy, who was holding the pads, noticed her watching and offered her a quick nod. Ila refocused as Michael directed her out toward the cage.

The first major step on her journey had begun.

*

Stuffy with heat and the stench of sweat, the hall was already a furnace. And this was only the first fight? The crowd was like nothing she'd fought in front of before. They screamed and banged on the back of the chairs. Unlike the respectful applause that had accompanied her last fight, this was like the coliseum of ancient Rome.

Blocking it all out as the fight began, she focused only on her opponent.

Valdez was stout and quick. Her eyes fixed on Ila in a hateful stare.

She stayed relaxed as Valdez continued to whip her with kicks and punches to gauge her range.

Michael's yelled instructions from their corner were lost in the cacophony of the crowd. But it didn't matter because she could decipher Valdez's game. It was the same as hers. She was looking for an opening to take the fight to the ground.

There wasn't much time left in the first round, and neither had made much headway on the scorecards.

Then it happened.

Valdez shot to one knee and drove forward, taking both of Ila's legs out from under her.

She was driven into the mat. She tried to turn on to her side to block Valdez's attack, but she wasn't fast enough.

Valdez flattened her on her back and delivered three horrifyingly fast hammer fists to Ila's face. Now Valdez was in front on the score sheet and Ila's nose was spilling blood.

Covering up as her opponent continued to batter away at her, Ila knew she had to get off her back, and counterattack. If she could make it to the end of the round, then she could reset for the next.

Valdez shifted her weight, only for a second, yet it was enough time for Ila to bridge her hips, launching Valdez off her.

Catching her shoulder, Ila dragged the woman down. Valdez cursed in frustration. Ila was on her back, sliding her arm around her opponent's neck. But Valdez wasn't beaten just yet. Ila had the choke locked in, but Valdez had her hands on Ila's arm preventing her from squeezing down on her neck.

"Ila!" She heard Michael yell, his voice just audible above the crowd. "You've got twenty seconds! Push for the submission!"

Ila strained to close the choke. Valdez resisted with everything she had. However, centimeter by painful centimeter, Ila closed the gap, and squeezed down on her adversary's throat.

Yet still, Valdez refused to tap out!

Ila's arms were becoming heavy as the lactic acid filled them, but finally Valdez went limp.

"She's out!" the referee yelled, waving his hands to signal the fight was over.

Ila rolled away, and lay on her back utterly exhausted. It had only been one round, under three minutes of action, but it had been a hell of a fight.

Michael appeared and yanked her to her feet. "One down!" he shouted, "Easy money!"

Michael beamed with excitement but she shook her head at him. "About as easy as wrestling a bus!" He laughed helping her from the cage.

Back in the change rooms the medical team looked her over and gave her the all-clear but the fight had sapped so much from her. Things were only going to get worse from here too.

Ila closed her eyes, focusing on her reasons, why.

*

A tap on her shoulder, and she opened her eyes to find the kid from the North Side gym, Rose, was gazing down on her as she lay on the change room bench.

"Just wanted to say good work on your fight," Rose said.

Ila sat up. "Thanks. You up soon?"

She nodded. "I hope you lose your next one," Rose said flatly.

Ila frowned.

"That way I won't have to worry about being choked into sleepy land," she continued with a chuckle.

Ila gave a tired laugh. "Well, hopefully *you* lose. Then I won't have to worry about that nasty front kick of yours."

Cathy beckoned Rose over. She gave Ila a nod and headed off.

Watching the kid shadow spar as she walked to her coach, she noticed how quick and smooth her strikes were. But the chink in the kid's armor was a big one, her lack of ground fighting knowledge. Mixed Martial Arts was a three-sixty and up and down fight. Rose would be taken apart if the fight went to the ground.

The official popped his head around the door again. "Fight three, Tanner versus Parker! Fighters to the cage."

Ila watched Cathy gather up her corner gear and usher an extremely nervous looking Rose to the door.

As they passed, Ila called to her. "Watch that Parker girl, she comes out hard."

Rose offered a nod of thanks and walked on. Ila had a nagging feeling that she would end up fighting Rose. Sure, she looked nervous, but she also looked at home here in this mini coliseum.

CHAPTER 50

t quickly degenerated into an utter slugfest as both Rose and Parker came out all guns blazing, and the crowd had roared at the spectacle.

Cathy's instructions to keep the fight standing and continuing to move had worked so far. It also seemed that Parker wanted to avoid the ground fight as much as possible.

Both were tiring from the frantic pace yet Rose was fading faster, and Parker knew it.

Catching Rose in a clinch against the cage, Parker fired off a knee strike to Rose's ribs. But the strike, although horribly painful, sparked new energy into Rose. Breaking the clinch, and shoving Parker back, Rose delivered her devastating front kick to the woman's stomach. She reeled back, clutching at her gut.

Rose used the opportunity to try and smash the woman's legs out from under her. She threw a low, clumsy yet vicious kick at Parker's leg. It connected sharply right on the side of her opponent's knee.

Parker howled and dropped to the canvas, clutching at the joint.

"Top position!" Cathy ordered. Rose was about to leap on top of Parker and batter the girl. She had her! All she had to do was land a few solid strikes and the referee would stop the fight.

The sight of Parker riving on the ground seemed familiar. *Tierney.*

She looked to the official then down at the agony etched on the girl's face.

The ref noticed her glancing at him. "What are you doing? Engage!" he said gesturing to the fallen fighter.

"She's done!" Rose protested.

He looked down at Parker. "Do you want to stop?" Parker shook her head and struggled to come to standing. But collapsed again, unable to put any weight on her battered leg

Rose scanned the crowd baying for her to finish the girl off. Cathy was gesturing angrily at her to pummel the fallen opponent, and Parker's own corner were screaming at her to get up.

Rose stepped to the referee and grabbed him by the shirt. "Look at her! She's done!"

He glared back at her, and seemed about ready to give her an earful, but then he looked to the riving fighter. His eyes softened slightly. "Please," Rose insisted. "It's enough!"

He waved his hands above his head, signaling the end of the fight. Rose sighed with relief. All she could see in her mind's eye was the broken face of Tierney.

Cathy whacked the cage angrily. "What the hell was that?"

"She was done!"

"You think she would've done the same for you?"

"No," said Rose in a cold voice. "She wouldn't have, that's the difference."

Cathy wasn't happy though. "Next time, make sure it's done. And for God's sake, kid, don't touch the ref! Come on, we got to get you iced up for the next fight."

*

Behind the curtain of the fighter's entrance, Ila had watched everything unfold. The fight had been frenetic, and she could see that Rose had developed into a formidable stand-up fighter, but she'd never seen a fighter hold off on finishing an opponent like that before. She turned back into the change room. That was all she needed to see.

CHAPTER 51

Ila landed jarringly on the mat, pain whipping through her body. Gazing up at her opponent, who had introduced herself as Angela in the change rooms, she remembered how friendly the woman had seemed.

Kindness certainly didn't equal weakness, she mused. Angela was tossing Ila around the cage like a rag doll.

Strong and quick, plus a grappler to boot, Angela continued to counter all of Ila's attempts at a takedown. For two rounds Angela had bested her. Now she covered up as Angela went for the ground assault. The punches were coming down too fast and hard for her to attempt a bridge escape.

"You ok in there?" the referee yelled. She shot him a thumbs up in the split second between being pummeled.

The bell sounded. Angela leapt up and moved off to her corner with a calm gait. It was like she'd just been told to take lunch during her workday.

As Ila came dizzily to standing, the ref walked her to her corner grabbing Michael's attention as he approached. "Listen, if she keeps taking punishment, I have to stop the fight."

Michael waved him off and sat her down on the stool. He

began cleaning up her cuts as he spoke. "You're well behind on points. You have to keep the fight standing," he stated.

"Standing?" she asked incredulously. "I thought the whole plan was to go to ground?"

"Every take down you've tried, she's reversed it. Then you end up trapped with her smashing you."

The crowd erupted as the announcer called through the sound system, "Third and final round!"

Michael paused for the noise to subside a tad then continued. "It's clear you can't beat her on the ground. You need to do something she's not going to expect. No takedowns!"

The referee called the fighters to their feet. His instruction went against everything they'd planned. The doubt in her face must have been clear. Gripping her by the shoulders. "Stand up and back yourself."

He was waved out of the cage by the referee as the bell sounded.

Ila attempted to throw her combinations. Angela slipped them and tackled her to the ground. On her way down, she caught a look at Michael, his head in his hands.

The whole round was just an endless grind.

Angela beat on her relentlessly. Now stuck on her back with defeat in sight, Ila had to dig down again into her reasons why she was here. When two opponents were so evenly matched, maybe the only thing that could separate them was their mental fortitude. She decided that if she were to be beaten, it would be on her feet. Bridging her hips hard, she rolled so that Angela tumbled off her.

The two leapt to standing again, and Ila, knowing full well that Angela had probably done enough to win on points, went on the attack.

Picking her shots, as Angela backed away, it became clear she was running down the clock. Ila's instinct took over.

Sliding low, she surprised herself as she nailed the takedown.

Angela covered up however, as the round ticked down to an end.

But Ila fought for the submission, and managed to flatten Angela on her back, grab her wrist and stretch her arm from her body.

She then forced her other arm under Angela's, gripped her own wrist and twisted, forcing the Kimora submission.

Angela howled in pain and instantly tapped out. There was only eight seconds left on the clock when the referee waved off the fight.

There was no celebration though. Both fighters lay there panting and exhausted.

She felt Michael's hands pulling her up to sitting. "I thought I told you to keep the fight on your feet?" he said angrily. But a grin slipped across his lips. "What the hell would I know anyway?"

They shared a laugh, enjoying the hard-fought win.

Ila was now into the final. But whomever she would be coming up against would be at their peak too, and despite her show of spirit, Ila wondered if she had anything left inside to get her over the line.

CHAPTER 52

Reclining on the bench against the wall while Cathy rubbed down her sore and beaten muscles, Rose meditated on her journey to this moment. Wincing as Cathy touched an extremely sore spot on her ribs, Cathy asked, "Did you catch that in the fight?" as she applied an ice pack to the area.

Rose shook her head.

"Walk into another door?"

They shared a slim smile.

"Listen," Cathy's tone became serious. "I called David about your situation."

Rose felt a sudden pang of dread rush through her. She wasn't exactly sure why though. Hadn't she stood up to her father already? Wasn't this the beginning of putting him behind her, and moving forward?

Cathy noted Rose's shock but continued calmly. "David said the cops had already forwarded a report from a family member to him. Said this family member has agreed to lay charges."

It had to be Jo. Her step-mum had made the move, and finally separated from him. But this dance had been danced before. It remained to be seen if he was really out of their lives.

Cathy continued. "It takes balls to do what you did. To stand up to someone like that and ask for help."

A million different thoughts ran through her mind. She sensed Cathy pondering silently. She spoke as though to herself, and Rose had the sense that this was no longer about her or Cathy.

It was about *them*, together.

"When I was competing... feels like ten thousand years ago now, my dad used to tell me to go out and fight like it was my last stand. He drilled that into me."

Rose nodded, gritting her teeth. She could feel the fuel to fight returning. "But I don't want you to do that," Cathy said kindly, almost dismissively. "I want you to go out there and fight for your new life." She stood, offering her hand. Rose took it and Cathy yanked her to her feet. "Are you ready for your new life?"

Rose slipped her mouth guard in, and cracked her knuckles.

*

Before she could defend, Rose found herself flipped to the ground. Her adversary dived on top of her, throwing down heavy fists.

Jenna, her opponent, was a methodical and resilient fighter. This was going to be one hell of a struggle.

Bridging her hips, she launched Jenna off her, and the two rolled to standing and began trading blows.

Jenna lunged forward and caught Rose in a clinch against the cage, and attempted a sweep but Rose defended.

The bell rang, signaling the end of the round, and Jenna

threw a frustrated upper cut, catching her on the chin. Her head rocked back sharply, stars flashed in Rose's vision.

The referee split them apart then shoved Jenna toward her corner. "You pull that shit again, and you're disqualified!" he yelled.

"I didn't hear the bell!" she protested.

Cathy clambered over the cage, to remonstrate with the referee about Jenna's cheap shot.

Finally, after she and the official gave each other an ear bashing, Cathy returned to the corner where Rose sat. "You good?" Cathy asked.

She nodded. The punch had rattled her, but she was feeling surprisingly energised.

"You need to move your head after you throw a punch," Cathy was saying. "When she goes for that take..." but Cathy's voice slipped into the cacophony of noise around the cage. Rose's eyes wandered out to the crowd, her vision still blurry.

A mass of strange faces watched on. Some cheered and laughed. Some were simply talking among each other, hardly even glancing at the cage.

But one concerned face locked eyes with her.

Rose jerked up straight. Petra gave her nervous yet encouraging eyes.

"Fighters up!" the referee called.

"Remember, combos! You have to start putting your strikes together," Cathy yelled.

The fighters stood.

The bell sounded.

The final round began.

*

Michael and Ila slipped from the change room to watch the final round of Rose's fight. Ila was developing a soft spot for the trainer and kid. They were underdogs, and hard fighters, both.

Ila didn't know much about Rose, other than the fact that she was clearly a tough kid who possessed a fighting spirit that wasn't glorious or, honestly, even that skillful. But the kid was a fast learner and clearly used to scrapping.

They observed the final round in considered silence. Rose was throwing her combinations effectively, and. And although her opponent was often quicker to the punch, Rose's defense was holding strong.

It was an extremely close fight.

Rose delivered a blink-and-you'll-miss-it leg kick that sent her opponent staggering.

"She's improving every fight," Michael commented.

Ila nodded; it was true. Rose was learning and probably didn't even realise it. But her opponent tackled Rose to the ground.

Ila screamed out for her to sprawl, but the cry was lost in the roar of the crowd. Rose defended well enough but couldn't get back to her feet.

For the remainder of the round, her opponent grappled and punched her. When the bell sounded, Ila and Michael shared a disappointed shrug, and returned to the change rooms.

The kid had performed bravely, but her opponent had

clearly done enough to secure a comfortable points victory.

For all her hard work, the kid had fallen short.

CHAPTER 53

The change rooms sat mysteriously dark and empty, all the losing fighters having packed up and left. Rose would join them soon. The weight of the days fighting, and the pressure had fallen on Rose, leaving her in almost catatonic state exhaustion.

She wasn't even sure now if she had seen Petra out there or if it had all been a cruel mirage her mind had conjured to give her hope.

Cathy unwrapped her hands, checking her over for any injuries. The grizzled coach was still fuming over the upper cut that Jenna had landed after the bell.

"We should contest the decision," she muttered grimly.

But Rose just sniffed and gave a weary grin. "It won't make any difference," she said.

Cathy gave a defeated nod and plopped down next to her.

"I'm sorry I lost your gym," Rose said sadly.

Cathy gave a shake of her head. "Don't talk rubbish. That was all me and my brilliant, drunken decision making."

"But where are we going to train?" Rose asked. Cathy frowned, dark eyes questioning beneath the crimson bandana.

Rose slapped her on the leg, "You didn't think we'd call it quits after this little setback, did you?" she said.

Cathy offered a generous and excited smile. But then she looked past Rose.

Rose turned to see what had caught the coach's attention. Her breath deserted her instantly. Petra was there in the doorway, her eyes inviting but nervous. She was dressed in jeans and a plain top; no makeup, and her hair tied back in a ponytail.

Rose had never seen her friend without any bells and whistles on.

Petra rung her hands as she spoke. "Hi... I just... just wanted to say hello." Her voice was not the loud, confident baritone it usually was.

Cathy raised an eyebrow to Rose. "Ah... right... I'll um, just grab some ice for your bruises." She winked at Rose and left the room.

They stood awkwardly before each other. It was Petra who spoke first picking up one of Rose's fight gloves as she did. "A cage fighter, hey? That's so you," she said.

But Rose didn't want to indulge in small talk. There were things she needed to say before her courage left her. "P... I... I just want to say I'm sorry about what I did—"

Petra raised her hand. "No. I thought that you wanted something from me that I couldn't give you. I panicked. *I'm* sorry."

Rose moved and took hold of her shoulders. "You've been the one fucking thing in my life that's been good. I thought I'd lost you."

Petra reached up to take Rose's hands in her own. "You could've told me you know... if you were... you know... like that," she said with a shrug.

She picked up on Petra's meaning. There was so much she wanted to say to her dark-haired, wild Turkish girl, but she calmed herself and just enjoyed the fact Petra was here. "Does it matter to you if I am... you know... like that?" she said shyly.

Petra adjusted her ponytail in thought for a moment. Then the mischievous smile split her face. "Well, Rosie, you know I can't really blame you, I mean, I am all that, and as I've said before you are just a basic bitch after all. I'm surprised that you lasted so long without making a move."

Rose laughed, playfully pushing Petra. "You really are a shit, you know that?"

"Well, you're a shit kisser," she retorted without missing a beat.

Rose swept her up in a gentle hug feeling Petra's arms wrap tightly around her. She didn't care that she'd lost her fight, or that there was uncertain times ahead for her. All that mattered was she had her friend back.

Petra pushed her away, screwing up her face as she did. "You fucking stink by the way! I'm surprised that girl you were fighting didn't tap out from your wiff!"

They both broke into laughter and hugged again. Cathy burst back into the room, panting and flustered.

"You need to come with me right now, kid!"

CHAPTER 54

Michael, Ila, Rose and Cathy mingled in a small meeting room with the head officials from the tournament. The main official was before them. Sweat drenched his tight suit and peppered his forehead. It had been a long day for him, that much was evident.

Ila was surprised to see Rose and Cathy. She'd assumed that whatever was going on it would have to do with the remaining two fighters.

"Jenna Tua can't fight. Her knee is wrecked from that kick you gave her," the official said, nodding to Rose.

Michael stepped forward. "So, if she forfeits, then we win!" he rejoiced.

But the official shook his head. "Not yet. Under the rules the eliminated fighter with the most points can advance to the final match up if one of the finalists has to withdraw."

He spun to face Rose, and Ila understood what was happening. "That's where you come in, Tanner. You had the highest amount of points from your two fights. But it's entirely your call."

All eyes fell to the kid. It was clear she was struggling to decide.

Ila hoped that Rose wouldn't agree to advance to the final. Ila really didn't want to have to beat her up. But if the kid was all that stood between her and ten thousand dollars, as well as the prestige of winning the brutal, Warrior Heart tournament, well, she wasn't going to go easy on her. All she had to do was, take the fight to the ground, submit her, and take home the prize. It would be the first step on the next leg of her journey to the big leagues.

The kid's eyes flashed to her, and she gave Rose a shrug as if to say, 'It's your call, and yours alone.'

But those questioning eyes seemed to ask, 'Should I?'

Ila nodded. As much as she'd like to walk away with the money right there and then, the martial artist in her wanted to take it fairly.

Rose gave her the smallest suggestion of a thankful nod, and turned to the official. "Ok," she said.

"You're in?" the official confirmed.

"Yes."

He rubbed his hands together. "Fantastic! We'll get medical to clear you and then we proceed with the final bout. Good luck, ladies."

He moved off and Rose slipped out with Cathy. Ila felt Michael's arm slide around her waist, "Easy money," he whispered in her ear.

She took his hand and held it to her chest. "Unlikely."

CHAPTER 55

The fading afternoon light spilled through the high, wire-coated window in Abdul's cell. The sun dipped out of sight. The shadows in the cell grew heavy. His thoughts grew heavy with them.

Was this going to be his life now and ever after?

His lawyer had been straight with him, explaining it was highly unlikely he would escape jail time. Given everything else he'd done, and the amount of times he'd been arrested, not to count the amount of times Abdul had been given formal cautions. It was certain he would be spending a lot more time inside walls like these.

What hurt more than the prospect of going to jail, was the fact that none of the boys had come to see him.

None of them!

Only Ila had physically been there for him. She was the only one that had given a fuck. Well, that was how it felt to him.

He was seventeen, almost eighteen, and maybe the only thing that would work in his favor, was the fact that he was under the age to be tried as an adult. He lay down on the solid, metal bed with its rubber mattress.

With the fall of the light, the temperature had fallen too. His breath misted in the frosty air of the cell. Closing his eyes, he thought of his sister. She'd be at her competition right now. He suddenly wished he were there to see it. That had been her dream, and she made it reality.

Perhaps he needed to start thinking about what sort of reality he wanted to live. His hands clenched as he curled up on the bed. *I've let her down. She was the only one that gave a shit. I should be there with her today.*

Within the stark cell, as the shadows closed in on him, Abdul made a promise to his sister and to himself. When he got out again, he would be there for her, the way she'd been there for him.

It wouldn't be easy turning things around. In fact, it would be near impossible.

But he would do it.

The alternative was to end up back here again and again, and for what? Having a rep with his boys? They didn't care, not really. But Ila did, and he'd let her down.

"Not again," he whispered to himself.

The sun was gone, and night was coming.

It would be long, lonely and the first of many.

CHAPTER 56

J o watched him being led to the police car through the opened front door. He kept looking back with pleading eyes but soon he was locked in the back and the car drove away.

She held Beth to her as she sat on the couch. The child was wriggling to get away and reaching for that stupid wind-up toy she always played with.

Two cops sat before her, one asking questions and the other was busy scribbling notes on a pad. Cops made her nervous, they always had, and she didn't like them in her house. She'd never trusted them. They'd always been seen as something to be wary of. And certainly, you never talked or ratted someone out to them. That was what she'd been taught as a kid.

But this was different.

Nathan was becoming more violent with Rose, and she was terrified that it would only be a matter of time before he turned his rage on Bethany. She squeezed her daughter closer, not wanting to let her slip away. The very thought of being alone with the girls now scared her to death. Was this something she could really do? Look after two kids?

Nathan always told her that they needed each other. That they were a team, and that he needed her as much as she needed him. Her reflection blinked at her in the window, as a cloud passed over the late afternoon sun. The woman who gazed sadly back was not the woman she knew. This woman was broken by the beguiling lies pressed on her for years.

He'd beat her. He'd beat his own daughter. He manipulated her, and he lied. That was what hurt so deeply. He lied, always promising things would change. That *he* would change.

Nothing ever did.

"Joanne?"

She blinked at the cop sitting opposite her.

"Did you hear me?" he asked gently.

She shook her head as Bethany finally slipped out of her grip and retrieved her wind-up car from the ground.

"I asked if you wanted us to go ahead and press charges on Nathan?" he said.

Bethany held out the car to the policeman writing notes. He grinned and ruffled her hair.

In that brief moment that she gazed at her daughter, she thought of Rosie as well. It had been a brave thing for her to stand up to her dad. After all, she'd been dealing with him her whole life.

Was it time to back herself the way Rosie had done?

"Joanne?" the policeman asked again, his voice tinted with frustration.

She nodded. "Yes. Yes, I want to press charges."

He turned to his partner. As they went over their notes,

Beth reached up and took her hand. Jo looked down at her in surprise. "What is it, love?"

Beth pressed the toy car into her hand.

Jo's resolve broke and her tears fell. But they were not tears of fear or sadness. They were tears of freedom and hope for her new life with her daughters.

CHAPTER 57

The woman he had chosen to spend the rest of his life with sat at the kitchen table. His beautiful twins, Mohammed and Evie, were sitting opposite their mother, listening intently as she helped them with their homework.

Amir observed from the darkness of the hallway, the ghosts of the killings from which he'd fled still beating on his mind. Faces of family he'd lost swirled before him. It felt like the shadowed hallway was his private projector room, and the darkness was giving the memories a canvas.

But his eyes focused on the light of the kitchen. They took in the cheerful, innocent smiles of his babies.

The children had a future, all his children did.

Abdul?

He walked cautiously toward the light. Yes, Abdul *could* have a future, yet it was up to him what it would look like.

And it is up to me to offer guidance; I have done a poor job up until now.

Amir stopped in the doorway, and his children smiled up at him. Rita gazed uncertainly, however. After a hesitation, he took her hand. Rita sighed, and squeezed his in turn. In that moment, forgiveness was asked, and promises were made.

Amir smiled to himself; he had a lot of forgiveness to earn. But he felt a sense of relief and even triumph.

He had found his dream.

Now his children could follow their own.

CHAPTER 58

The bell sounded. A tremendous roar echoed through the hall. Ila felt it through her whole body.

She walked toward Rose, her fist extended to touch gloves, a show of respect for one another.

The moment their gloves touched, and they fell back into their fighting stances, a wave of focused silence fell on her. It felt as if they were the only two people in the world. The kid was moving confidently. It took Ila by surprise, and she knew that while there was no reason to change her game plan, this was certainly not going to be the quick finish she'd envisioned.

Rose was suddenly within striking range, and Ila wore clean and powerful strikes. But the kid over stretched, and Ila landed her own counter punches. She slipped Rose's jab and hit her with the straight right.

For the remainder of the first round, the two fighters traded punches. Rose threw far more, but Ila's counter shots were cleaner.

The bell sounded and the pair stopped and stared at each other for a moment. As they moved back to their corners, the roar of the crowd returned. It was like someone had turned the volume back up suddenly.

Ila dropped down on the stool. Her mind still focused. However, the pain from Rose's strikes was causing her body to quiver and throb with pain. She hadn't realised just how hard she'd been hit.

"Why are you standing up with her?" Michael cried with frustration.

She blinked at him. "What?"

"You didn't even try to get her to the ground! What are you thinking? We don't fight on the *opponent's* terms, we fight on *our* terms, remember? Bring her to the ground and end the fight! She's got no defense against it, and you know it."

*

Rose still felt strong despite the heavy counter strikes she'd taken. Cathy rubbed the ice bag on the back of her neck. "She's going to try and get you on the ground. So watch out for the take down, it's coming!"

Cathy took a deep breath, then continued, "So for fuck's sake, keep moving and—"

"Keep my fucking hands up?" Rose grinned.

Cathy clapped her on the shoulder. "Finally learning."

*

The bell sounded again, and Rose moved imposingly toward Ila like a seasoned veteran.

Gee, she really is a fast learner, Ila mused.

Every time she swooped in fast for Rose's legs, the kid would slip just out of reach.

But still, she was wearing her down tactically. Surely it

was only a matter of time before Ila would get the fight to the ground. She just had to be careful of the kid's strikes.

At last, the opportunity came.

Rose threw a flurry of shots and overreached again, this time with her front kick.

Ila slipped to the outside of the kick, caught Rose's leg and swept the other one out from under her.

Rose let out a cry of anger at being brought to the ground. Ila quickly gained control and pinned her on her back. The kid fought hard to escape, but the simple truth was, she just didn't have the skills.

Michael waved his hands as if to say, 'take your time.' Nodding her understanding, she set about wearing Rose down slowly. She began forcing Rose's arm behind her, and pressing her wrist back at a sickening angle. *Not long now.*

Then suddenly Rose grunted and threw her aside with one hand.

Ila tumbled. The crowd screamed in amazement.

By sheer will and strength, Rose had just shoved the dominant ground fighter off her like she was a doll.

They struggled up to their feet. For the first time, dread fell over her. Rose wasn't going down easy. And as the kid rampaged forward landing her strikes, Ila knew she was losing this fight.

The bell sounded and Rose stood before her, chest heaving, face blood red and waves of sweat spilling down her body.

"You're not making this easy, are you?" Ila muttered.

Rose offered a nasty grin. "Neither are you."

The referee pushed between them and guided them away to their corners.

*

Rose was spent. She genuinely had nothing left to give. Cathy was there again with the ice bag on Rose's neck, and for a good twenty-odd seconds she just held it there, and gave Rose a look she couldn't quite read.

"Just breathe, kid," Cathy said calmly. "She's good but she only has one game plan."

"I can't beat her down there!" Rose spluttered between breaths. "It took everything I had just to get her off me. That fucking Jiu Jitsu shit!"

"Relax, kid," Cathy said. "You've gone further than anyone thought you could, even me. So, just go out there and give it everything you've got. Who cares if you win or not? Fight for you new life, remember?"

Rose slunk back against the cage, and the pressure slipped away. The fear of her father, the fear of losing Petra, and the pressure to win and save Cathy's gym, had all built up inside her and dragged at her. She hadn't even realised until this moment how much she was carrying on her shoulders.

Light and calm now, her breath returned. The bell sounded for the final round. She got up as the referee signaled for the coaches to exit the cage, but as she stepped forward for the last round, Cathy gripped her gloved hand. "Thank you, Rose."

"Huh? For what?"

But the grizzled coach just smiled. The grim eyes beneath

the red bandana were welling with tears. Cathy wiped them before they could form. "Hands up, kid, and you'll do fine."

*

This long day had finally caught up with her. She could barely hold her head up. And yet, she knew she could beat this girl. She just had to wear her down some more and get that submission hold.

Michael bashed on the cage to get her attention. She turned to look at the man she loved. He was passionate to see her succeed, and he would blame himself if she didn't.

He rattled off instructions frantically. The bell sounded for the last round, and she held out her hand to silence him. "It's all right," she said lovingly. "You've done enough. It's up to me."

She turned and headed into battle.

*

They came together in the center of the cage, the cheers of the crowd coming in waves of sound, crashing over them.

This was it.

If Rose could keep the fight standing, avoid the takedowns, she'd have a chance of winning on points.

She threw a jab, whipping the punch out toward Ila's chin, expecting to feel the satisfying thump of bone on bone.

But instead, Ila dropped her weight low, and rammed into Rose's hips, driving her to the ground again.

She groaned in pain, as Ila pinned her to the canvas. Rose scraped and pushed, trying everything to escape Ila's clutches. Ila was methodical in her attack this time, though. The moment

Rose tried to escape, Ila adjusted, wrapping her arm around Rose's neck, applying the rear naked choke. As she applied the pressure, Rose caught hold of Ila's arm, wrenching it as hard as she could off her throat.

There was an instant stalemate, as Ila couldn't completely land the choke, and Rose couldn't quite get Ila's arm from her neck.

The crowd's roar escalated to a deafening level. Rose thought the roof was going to cave in.

Slowly, Ila squeezed, but Rose could tell it was sapping every bit of her opponent's remaining strength. Rose's arms felt as if they had fire burning through them as she fought to stop the choke. But she managed to lift herself up on to all fours with Ila still on her back!

The announcer called, "Final thirty seconds!" over the sound system. The voices of the crowd lifted to a fever pitch.

*

"Just tap out! It's over!" Ila hissed into Rose's ear. But the kid gritted her teeth. The girl just wasn't going to give up. She would have to try something else.

To the shock of the crowd, she released her chokehold. Rose breathed in huge gasps.

Ila rolled Rose on to her back, and dropped on to her stomach, pressing her weight down and pinning her in place.

If she simply landed a few well-aimed punches, the referee would stop the fight. She felt him hovering over her shoulder, waiting to dive in and save Rose from any more punishment.

The problem was, the kid was holding on well, despite

her exhaustion.

Ila raised her fist to strike.

Rose's blood shot eyes gazed at her defeated, but she covered her head with her arms.

Ila paused. Her fist gripped above her head. They were all screaming at her to finish the kid off.

The crowd hooted for blood. Even the referee was telling her, "You must engage! You can't just sit there!"

Ila looked across the cage at Cathy. The coach had her red bandana scrunched in her hand. Twisting it like rosary beads. Then her eyes fell back to the kid, covering up on the floor.

Her fist lowered.

Her arms heavy, like chains hanging at her sides. Sweat stung her eyes. The kid looked back at her, clearly longing for the bell to sound.

But it wasn't pity she felt for Rose. She reflected that she, Ila, was living her dream of being a fighter and that this was what her family had fought to give her. Here was someone fighting their own battle, and chasing their own dream.

Was it more than that though? Rose had earned her respect. Because fighting wasn't all about technique and combinations, it was something deeper.

Stepping off Rose, she knelt and slapped the canvas twice.

Everyone stopped and stared. The crowd's roar dulled, and the officials at their tabled glanced at each other in confusion. Even Rose frowned up at her. Only the referee seemed to understand what she was doing.

"Are you sure?" he stammered in disbelief.

She slapped the canvas again. "I'm tapping out," she announced.

He looked to the official's table. Collectively they all shrugged back at him.

"But... if you tap out, you'll lose!"

"I know." She tapped again.

The referee paused, then waved off the fight. There was a mix of moans, but also cheers in the crowd. Michael was looking at her, stunned. His mouth hung open. But she offered a loving smile with her eyes, and after a moment, he nodded his understanding.

She reached out her hand to Rose, who was still flat on her back. The kid took it and Ila pulled her to her feet.

"Why'd you do that?"

She shrugged. "You've got heart," she said.

Rose's bruised and battered face looked her up and down. She embraced Ila. The pair was so exhausted they were both struggling to stay upright.

It was an embrace of respect and honor between two people who had just gone to war.

"Well," Rose said as she released her. "That's another thing we have in common."

She raised Ila's arm to the crowd. They roared in return.

Ila's gaze fell on Cathy, who grinned up at them as she tied her bandana back around her head.

The old coach just folded her arms and gave her a single nod, which from Cathy, was as close to a hug and kiss on the cheek that anyone could hope for.

CHAPTER 59

Never could she have imagined that taking another urchin troublemaker in to her gym, her home really, could change the trajectory of her life so quickly.

Parked behind the desk, watching Rose mop the entrance area, she felt the pull of this new path. Rose hadn't won. But as Ila had said to them, it wasn't about gifting Rose the money or the win, it was about respect.

A respect that Ila insisted Rose had earned.

In the change room after the fight, the girls, Michael, and herself had spoken and hatched a plan.

For Cathy, this was both exciting and terrifying. This idea they'd come up with would be a huge step for her. It would mean the end of an era for her. Every time she thought about it, butterflies would dance around her stomach, and a weighty sense of dread slid onto her shoulders.

The front door of the gym swung open and both she and Rose were snapped from their thoughts. Cathy's heart pumped with anxiety when she saw who entered, but she held her usual steely gaze.

"Ladies!" Angelo boomed. He was looking relaxed and

fresh. He hadn't even bothered to bring his goons with him this time. He turned to Rose, slapping her solidly on the shoulder. "Congratulations on the win, kid! I tell you what though, that black chick must have a crush on you, huh? She certainly had you beat!"

He leered at Rose, who answered it with a stare as dark as midnight. "Maybe she likes a taste of that fresh, pale meat," he said, bursting into breathy laughter.

Cathy saw Rose's knuckles whiten on the mop handle.

Her teeth revealed in a sneer.

Cathy gave her a subtle nod. Her way of just telling Rose to relax.

Angelo looked between them. "Gee, bloody gloomy bunch you lot are. Anyway, I saw the video of your fight on the Internet. A real barnstormer! But I tell you what, people are loving what happened at the end there." He smiled openly at them, but neither said anything. Cathy was rather over Angelo strolling into her gym and causing her grief.

When he still got no response from them, he shrugged dismissively. "Anyway, it's that time, Bomber." He held out his hand. "You got what I need?"

She gave a stiff nod.

"Well thank goodness for that. Now we can finally put all this nastiness behind us and move on. I really did find this all so upsetting," he continued, his expression a fake mask of sympathy. "I mean, your father and I, we were so close back in the day and—"

"If you mention my dad one more time, I'm going to leap

this counter and rip your arms off!"

His genial expression dropped. It seemed to Cathy, he had the sudden realization that maybe he should have brought his thugs along with him after all. But he straightened his jacket and folded his arms. "Just give me what I want, Bomber."

Reaching under the desk, she produced a set of keys and tossed them to him.

He looked from the keys to her in anger. "What the hell is this?"

"The keys to the building. That's what you really wanted, wasn't it?" she cast a hand to the gym. "Now you can turn that profit you keep drooling over."

His eyes twinkled and she could almost see the dollar signs in them. "You'd give up your father's legacy rather than just hand over the money?"

"This gym isn't my dad's legacy." She tapped her chest. "I am. And I'm going to take it to the next level."

Angelo scoffed. "But the cash—"

"The money is for Rose and her family." She flashed a smile at the kid. "It's time for them to create a new legacy too."

Angelo tossed the keys happily. "Yeah whatever. I'll have this place in the hands of developers within a month, and then you'll see what *real* money looks like."

"I'll email you the deed tonight. I hope this makes you happy, Ange," she said. "As you said, its only bricks and mortar."

But he wasn't listening. A grotesque smile was plastered on his face. She could just see him imagining the block of flats that he'd get developed. "Be seeing you, Bomber," he said.

"You better hope not."

But he was out the door and on his phone already. No doubt to start the calls to develop the property.

"Should've smashed him," Rose said, as if she was commenting on something as casual as turning on a tap.

She scoffed. "You can't just go around punching every problem you have in the face, remember?"

"Can't we make an exception just once?"

CHAPTER 60

R ose held the door to the – what had Ila called it? Dojo? – open for Cathy as she battled with the bags of equipment they'd salvaged from the gym. The rest they sold for scrap, or to the handful of members still at the gym.

Walking through the Dojo toward the large, matted area, the sound of people training, the smell of sweat and the heavy atmosphere in the air was both exciting and, Rose had to admit, intimidating.

Standing awkwardly for a moment they watched the session. Spotting Ila in the throng of people flipping and wrestling each other, she gave her a nervous wave. Ila beamed at her and called out to Michael, who was busy demonstrating some technique to a pair of students.

Jogging over to greet them, a few of the students gave them enquiring looks.

Rose felt Cathy let out a long sigh. "Relax," Rose whispered. "It's nothing you haven't done be for. It's just a new place."

"I know that." Cathy rolled her eyes. "I'm still bloody nervous though!"

Michael beamed his boyish smile. "Welcome guys, you ready to get started?"

Cathy stifled a cough, it was clear she was nervous to all present. "Yeah, can't wait!" she stuttered, but Michael gave her an understanding nod. "Listen, Michael, could I have a quick word?"

"Sure. Hey, Ila, why don't you get our latest white belt ready?"

Ila took Rose by the hand. "You ready to throw down?" she asked, leading her toward the change rooms.

"Only if it's on you!" she said giving Ila a playful bump.

Her new friend laughed. "Well, I'm not tapping out this time, so be ready."

As Ila pushed the door open, Rose looked back to Cathy; the woman had shown her so much, and now they were both stepping onto a new journey. Cathy's anxiety was branded on her face, but she'd be fine. Rose knew they both would. The brutal obstacles they'd faced in their lives hadn't beaten them. It had strengthened them.

Rose closed the door to the change rooms with a warm flutter in her chest. Ila held out a white belt to her. On a hook behind her hung a new Gi. It had a small Rose sewn on the lapel.

"Here, is where the journey starts," Ila said.

"Here, is where it *continues,*" Rose corrected, taking the belt.

Ila smiled. "I'll let you get changed. Remember, I'm not tapping out this time," she said as she walked past Rose.

Rose caressed the white belt, then reached out and traced the rose on her Gi. *The journey doesn't just continue, it never ends.*

CHAPTER 61

A nd this is the office," Michael said leading her into a small room off to the side of the training area, with a window looking out on to the mats. "I set up a desk for you." He gestured to a small desk in the corner. "It's not much, but feel free to make it your own."

"Cheers," she said softly.

"You ok?" he asked.

"No, I'm shitting myself. I haven't ever trained anyone outside of my dad's gym. Never known anything different!"

He gazed thoughtfully for a moment, and then closed the door. The din from the training area muffled, and Michael perched on his own desk. "Cathy, what you did with that kid was outstanding. You took her from some street scrapper to a fighter in no time." He threw his arms wide in disbelief. "Jesus, if Ila wasn't such a good grappler, we'd probably have lost that fight on points." With his eyes holding hers, he continued. "I don't have that level of striking knowledge. I don't think anyone has the experience that you do. Ila needs to learn it from you, and Rose needs to learn how to fight on the ground."

He clapped his hands together. "You ready to make these

girls into champions?"

She took a long breath and held out her hand. He gripped it in a firm shake.

"Welcome aboard, coach," Michael beamed. "I need to get back out there. But I mean it when I say make yourself at home. You're our new striking coach after all."

He hopped off the desk and skipped out of the room to bark instructions at his students.

Cathy realised she'd been holding her breath, and released a long sigh. This was a good job he was offering her. She'd be taking a class every night and helping get the fighters up to speed with their striking. She'd even found a small place to rent down the road. Sure, there was no furniture in it, and the heating didn't work. But it was a start. The slate was clean. She had started again, and this time her path was clear.

Reaching into her bag, she dug out the picture of her dad with his arm around her. Wiping a thin layer of dust from the glass, she placed it on the corner of her desk.

For a second it was all too much. The change, the loss of the gym, this new life, all of it sent her spiraling into emotions she'd held down for so long, but then she spotted Rose walking from the change room. Ila helped fix her belt, which she'd clearly tied wrong.

Cathy observed the two as they ran through some drills, giggling as Rose twisted and fell in an awkward heap.

Ila crashed into her. She reached out to grab Rose, but her hand accidentally smacked her hard across the face.

Kicking the desk angrily, she lurched to her feet. She threw open the door to the office, "Hey!" she boomed at Rose. Every face in the training area turned to her. The room went instantly silent.

"Keep your fucking hands up!"

ACKNOWLEDGEMENTS

My deepest thanks must first go to the brilliant editor and all round fantastic human, Amanda J. Spedding at Phoenix Editing. Thank you for your generous advice, hard work and assistance in bringing this story to life.

A massive thank you to David Schembri, for delivering yet another killer cover design. Your hard work and support is hugely appreciated.

Finally to you dear reader! Wether you bought stole or borrowed this book.

Thank you, and enjoy!

ABOUT THE AUTHOR

Stefan was born and raised in Adelaide, and began his career as a graduate actor from the Victorian College of the Arts, and appeared in many professional theatre, film and TV roles.

He has previously released *Beyond the Boundary Fence*, *Until the Storm Passes*, and *Sick Little Puppies* (A collection of short stories with Simon J Green.)

In 2019 he wrote and produced the short film *Homecoming*, which can now be viewed free on YouTube.

He also wrote the feature film **AFTER THE END**, available on iTunes, and released in 2020.

HEART is Stefan's third book.

www.facebook.com/Stefan-Taylor-Authorscreenwriter